THE
SCREAMING
BUDDHA

Also by Robert J. Bowman

THE HOUSE OF BLUE LIGHTS

THE
SCREAMING
BUDDHA

Robert J. Bowman

St. Martin's Press • New York

Design by Basha Zapatka

Library of Congress Cataloging-in-Publication Data

Bowman, Robert J.
    The screaming Buddha / Robert J. Bowman.
        p.   cm.
    "A Thomas Dunne book."
    ISBN 0-312-11056-1
    1. Taxicab drivers—California—San Francisco—Fiction.
    2. San Francisco (Calif.)—Fiction.   I. Title.
    PS3552.08758S36   1994
    813'.54—dc20   94-2177   CIP

First edition: July 1994

10 9 8 7 6 5 4 3 2 1

For my mother
Marjory L. Bowman

Many thanks to Rick Gough, Meg O'Brien, and Sarah
Brown for their comments, criticism, and friendship.

And to Ro Leaphart for insights into importing, and a
fine sense of larceny.

THE
SCREAMING
BUDDHA

One

IT'S MY FIRST BIG DECISION OF THE DAY. Understand, I'm a little slow in the morning. Usually these things start around nine but toy people go to bed early. To think like kids they've got to live like kids. So they throw open the doors of the exhibit hall at seven-thirty, and I'm supposed to be thinking clearly. It's not the pressure I mind, the twenty people in line behind me. I can handle the pressure. What I can't stand is some fat hotel security guard tapping me on the shoulder while I'm trying to pick out the right doughnut.

"Excuse me, sir. Do you have a badge?"

I turn around. He's six foot three. I'm five-ten in wingtips, a hundred and fifty pounds. "Excuse me?"

"You need to be wearing your convention badge in the exhibit hall."

"Ah." I fish out a business card. "Press list."

"Press must register, sir."

The people in line are getting restless. They're in the early stages of caffeine withdrawal. "I'm planning to register. I was just getting a cup of coffee."

"I'll have to ask you to go to the registration booth."

1

It's no use arguing. Once in a while you get somebody who's really into his job. I slip the card back into my jacket and look suitably exasperated. The next guy in line shakes his head. What a world, we agree silently. I quit the doughnut line.

The guard watches as I leave the exhibit hall and head for the registration desk. As a last resort I could try to register. Usually all it takes is a business card. Here, I'll show you:

GLOBAL TRADE AND TRANSPORT

JACK SQUIRE

SENIOR EDITOR

But I like to avoid it. I melt into the crowd at registration and circle back toward the doors. The overzealous security man has lost interest in me. I've taken out a plastic badge holder and clipped it to my lapel. In the holder is another one of my business cards, good enough for most shows. I pass another guard who barely glances at me. I'm back at the pastry table in time for a raisin roll.

Duly fortified, I pour myself a cup of coffee and start roaming the exhibit hall. It's only about fifty booths in a space sliced off from the main ballroom by accordion walls. The chandelier looks like the mothership in *Close Encounters of the Third Kind*. The carpet pattern is designed to camouflage food spills. You crash enough hotel conventions, you notice these things.

I need to be gone in half an hour. I've got two more trade shows to check out before I decide where to have a free lunch. Five hours from now I'll be small-talking about toys, trucks, or electroplating. Wherever the food's hot and they don't check your credentials.

I breeze by the exhibits. A few tips. Never make eye contact unless you mean to stop. And never stop unless the booth is giving something away, a keychain or a notepad or a seat cushion for ball games. Occasionally you'll get handed the odd brochure or business card that comes in handy later.

The pickings here are pretty slim. You'd think a novelty show would be giving away novelties, but everything's for sale and nothing looks very novel. There's blood bags, severed fingers, fake vomit that would be invisible in the hotel carpet. One guy's selling combination puke and shit, it comes in three sizes, the biggest the size of a fourteen-inch pizza. I'm glad I finished the raisin roll.

Here's a doll that wets itself on voice command. You program in the magic word. Bodily fluids are in this year. I take a business card and move on.

I keep expecting some crazed salesman to squirt disappearing ink on the suit, ink that never really disappears. Let me tell you about the suit: it's absolutely critical. You can't skimp on quality. Mine's lightweight wool, silky to the touch, a subtle cross-hatch stripe that's blue or brown, depending on the light. A suit like that people take seriously. I'm thirty-one but without the suit I barely look twenty-one. I toss in a good pair of wingtips for another inch of height. Also I comb my hair and leave the gimme caps at home.

I hear music. It's coming from three booths down and sounds like a miniature calliope on Dexedrine. Standing in front of the booth is a middle-aged woman with a knitted shoulder bag and a tam-o'-shanter. She looks shocked.

I stand beside her at a table full of identical plastic figures. They're nine inches tall and rocking from side to side. The feet are big black cartoon shoes. The clothes are red shorts with suspenders and big yellow buttons. The faces are rubber monster faces which writhe and stretch like taffy. The ears are plastic mouse ears. Each creature holds a glowing axe. I recognize the music: "When the Saints Go Marching In."

"Uhnnh," says the woman, and walks off. I'm left alone

with this vision of Psycho Killers R Us. Somebody speaks.

"Twenty-percent discount on orders of two hundred or more."

Behind the monsters is a man in a chair. He has thinning gray hair, pink gray skin, and bags under his eyes. He's wearing a light gray poly-blend suit and a red EXHIBITOR badge on his skinny lapel. He looks miserable.

"What the hell," he says, blowing his nose into a cloth handkerchief. "Buy one, I'll give you the twenty percent."

I say no thanks and start moving away.

"What the hell. *Take* one. Take three. Anything to get rid of them."

He looks like he's going to cry. I pick up one of the creatures. The legs are moving and the face is throwing itself into hideous expressions. It's like trying to hold a giant plastic caterpillar. One that plays "When the Saints Go Marching In."

I'm looking for the off switch. "Great novelty item," the man says, but he doesn't believe it. I'm becoming attached to the thing. It'd go great on the shelf over my bed, between Sluggo and the Creature From the Black Lagoon. "Thanks," I say, wondering how long before the batteries die out.

I move on with my door prize. "Not exactly Mickey Mouse," he says.

"No," I say, although I'm thinking it's very Mickey Mouse, which is part of the attraction.

"I mean it was supposed to *be* Mickey Mouse."

I'm ten feet from the booth and he's still talking. I come back just to be polite. This is what I mean by not stopping. It's easy to get trapped.

"I order a hundred plastic Mickey Mouse dolls with lollipops who sway back and forth to 'It's a Small World.' That's what the demo did. What I get is this."

A whole new concept. Mickey Mouse as axe murderer. "Screwed up the order," I say.

"Naw, they didn't." He grips one of the rubber faces and pulls it right off. There are three rotating knobs which fit into little cups in back of the face. When the knobs move, the face stretches.

"They *were* Mickey faces," he says with disgust, working the monster face in his hand like a puppet. "Somebody slapped these on instead." He's moving the monster mouth in time with his own words. "Then they swap the lollipop for an axe. Why the music I can't figure out. Why that song."

I wonder, too. Everybody hates that song. I remember a jazz club in New Orleans with a sign on the wall: REQUESTS, 25 CENTS. SAINTS, $5. "But why the switch?"

"Copyright. Probably got raided by the Disney Gestapo. Had to move the merchandise and I got caught in the middle."

Those are definitely Mickey's suspenders and shoes. I wonder whether "It's a Small World" would be any less obnoxious. This sounds like a funeral band trapped on a runaway merry-go-round. "Is there a way to turn it off?"

"Twist the axe." He reaches over and shows me. The thing dies in my hand. "I mean it, I'll give you fifty percent off two hundred. Seventy-five off five. I'll pay *you* to take a thousand."

"Thought you only ordered a hundred."

He laughs. It's not a happy laugh. "Two cartons, pal, fifty to a carton. They shipped a whole container."

"So you got just the one box?"

He looks at me strangely. "I'm talking a *container*. Big and metal, twenty feet long, eight and a half feet tall. With thousands of these . . . things."

"Why not send them back?" Except mine.

Again that hollow laugh. "You know what it costs to ship a container back to Taiwan?" He squints at the business card on my lapel. "Yeah, you know."

I nod sagely. Joe International Trade Reporter. "Well," I say, and start moving away again.

"I mean one container was bad enough. Then they try fobbing *two* of the goddamn things off on me."

"Thought you said they shipped just one."

"Naw, the other one wasn't mine, papers got stuck together with chewing gum. Anyway I'm down at the warehouse eleven o'clock last night, order's supposed to be in three days ago, and I'm panicking 'cause the show starts this morning and I've got zilch for the booth. Some punks broke into my car last week and took all my samples. So Mickey Mouse is it. And I end up with *this*."

He grips one of the crooning monsters like he wants to smash it into the tabletop. "On top of which they try sticking me with this second container of something else entirely. I show 'em my papers to prove it's not mine"—in his other hand he waves around a bunch of documents—"and I get the hell out of there. I mean, how'm I supposed to haul away *two* containers? I only rented the one tractor."

I press a button and the battery compartment springs open. Two double-As. "So what happened to the second container?"

He shrugs. "Last I saw it was sitting on a chassis outside the Pier Street Warehouse, bunch of bozos standing around scratching their heads. Nobody coming to claim it. Customs didn't give a damn."

"Pier Street Warehouse . . ."

"Near Third. Middle of the block."

"Twenty-foot container . . ."

"Twenty foot long. Green. Just sitting there on the street. With God knows what inside."

I hold up Psycho Mickey like an Oscar and back away

from the booth. And here I'd thought my day was all set. Now I'm contemplating a radical revision of the Filofax. "Thanks," I say.

"I mean, where would I *put* it? Got no room for the one I got. Know where it is right now? Parked out front on the street. Somebody's probably ripping it off even as we speak. Jesus, I hope so. Listen, you sure you don't want to take a couple hundred . . ."

I'm out of earshot of his voice but the music dogs me all the way to the door. So does the security guard who rousted me at the doughnut table. He tries cutting me off so I go another way. Outside the street has come alive and the sun's shining right in my eyes. I can't help singing out loud.

I'm gonna be there in that number . . .

Two

I GET BACK IN MY TAXICAB. It's a '59 Checker Marathon, in case you haven't noticed. Built like a battleship and there's room for one, too. Although it rides a bit rough. I recommend you hold on to that grip above the door. Had it specially installed. Cheaper than seat belts.

Actually it's not a cab at all in the strictest sense. I don't line up at the big hotels to carry tourists in white shoes fifty feet to some overpriced restaurant. I don't spend hours sucking in carbon monoxide at the airport and swapping *Playboy*s with the other cabbies. Normally I don't pick anybody up at all, you just lucked out. I'm what you might call an Irregular Route Common Carrier. I heard the term at some transportation convention. They had much better stuff than the novelty show. This combination compass/digital clock, I got it there. Also got my business card turned into a laminated luggage tag.

I cruise over to Pier Street, just a few blocks from here. It's not the nicest part of Our Fair City, mostly industrial, lot of warehouses and abandoned cars. Hardly a soul around at night. Sure enough, the green container's parked on the street, mounted on a set of wheels they call a chassis. I learned that at another transportation show. Gave me the idea for the business cards.

I drive by without stopping. No point being noticed. What would a cab be doing in that part of town anyway? "Take us down to the warehouses, driver. We hear there's an exquisite dumpster down there. We read about it in *Our Fair City on Fifty Recycled Aluminum Cans a Day*." See what I mean?

There's a big padlock on the back doors of the container. I keep going south, toward the ballpark, to a neighborhood of little Monopoly houses with pastel paint jobs. Downtown looks all buffed and shiny in my rearview mirror, like the Porsche your neighbor spends all day polishing, and he never takes it out. It looks a hell of a lot nicer than Jerry Mack's truck. He parks it on the street, where the elements take their toll. If the fog doesn't get you the salt air will. But I decide not to mention it. If I'm too obnoxious he might not let me borrow the truck.

"Jer-*ree*!" I say as he opens the front door in a torn T-shirt and gym shorts. "Long time!"

He stares at me for a few seconds like he's still waking up. What's left of his hair is sticking out in all directions. He hasn't shaved for several days. Basically he looks like shit. Once again I hold my tongue. I could have been a diplomat.

I follow him into the living room. He throws himself into an understuffed easy chair and I take the couch. It's covered with a pattern of fat gray orchids which used to be pink. There's a redwood-burl coffee table and a couple of cheap landscapes from the artists in the park on Sunday. Plus my old favorite, the Blue Chip Stamp Conquistador.

"Jack," he says, rubbing his face.

"Lucky to find you home." Jerry spends more time in his truck than his one-bedroom house, and it shows. There's a sports bag in the middle of the living room, spewing clothes.

9

He yawns. "Goin' to Albuquerque tomorrow."

I go into the kitchen and start rattling around. "So you don't need the truck tonight."

His eyes go wide. "For what?"

"For about an hour. Probably less."

"Jesus." He stares at the bag on the floor and shakes his head. "I'm not even supposed to be seeing you."

"Jerry, at this time of the morning you're not seeing anything. It's all a beautiful dream, my friend." I fill a saucepan with tap water and start it boiling.

"Ain't no dream if you're taking the truck."

"Borrowing, Jerry. Borrowing the truck. Tell you what. I'll find you a new bulldog for the hood, how'd that be?"

Somebody keeps ripping off his bulldog hood ornament. It's a Mack truck, hence my nickname for him.

Jerry nods. I rinse out a couple of mugs and scoop three tablespoons of instant coffee into each one. Then a dash of cinnamon. I can't believe Jerry keeps cinnamon in his pantry. But people will surprise you.

"Brakes okay?" I ask.

Jerry grunts.

"Got enough gas?"

"It comes back full, Jack. You can get diesel at the station on the corner. And watch the gas gauge, it gets stuck sometimes."

"I won't need much gas." I look around Jerry's living room and start humming that damned song. His place reminds me of a mobile home. It's so small he could hook it up to his tractor, which isn't a bad idea. Only have to stop for gas and groceries.

"I don't know, Jer. Maybe I'll become a truck driver." I sing a couple of bars from "The Wanderer."

"You get piles."

So much for the romance of the road. I pour boiling water into the mugs. They've got matching cartoon drawings of

10

Vegas showgirls, circa 1953. I carry them into the living room and balance one on the arm of Jerry's chair. "Drink up," I say. "Got to stay alert."

Back in the cab I put on some Dead Kennedys to wipe "Saints" out of my brain. I roll up the windows and scream along. The day's gone gorgeous, deep blue sky with the faintest breeze and a few scraggly clouds. It's early spring and the wildflowers are in bloom.

The freeway's packed so I cut north on surface streets toward the nicer part of town. I've had it with conventions for the day. Know who I feel sorry for? People who can't change their plans at a moment's notice. People who can't turn on a dime.

Men and women with briefcases wave at my cab as I come up through the Financial District. I wave back. What a friendly town. I could drive around all day. But I've got to get out of the suit.

It takes about twenty minutes to reach my place in the Heights. The street's lined with private schools and thirty-room mansions with a spectacular view of the bay and the bridge and the rolling hills beyond. Sailboats are blowing around like scraps of colored paper. Home.

I punch the garage door opener at the top of the steep driveway at the same time I shift into neutral and coast down. By the time I hit bottom I'm going twenty miles an hour. The bottom of the garage door snaps my aerial back. I slam on the brakes to keep from smashing into the far wall. I stop with less than a foot to spare. Haven't missed yet.

I know I'm in perfect position because the orange Styrofoam 76 Unocal ball hanging from the ceiling is tapping the windshield. I climb out of the cab and activate the hydraulic lift. The car goes up ten feet. I use a drip pan to keep the oil off my bed.

Someone's banging on the side door. It's Putz Huffington,

11

the twelve-year-old kid from upstairs. His real name is McAllister. I'm the only one who calls him Putz. He comes down to read my comic books, play the CD, VCR, Nintendo.

He's wearing his Catholic school uniform. "You got the new *Judge Dredd*?"

"On the milk crate. What are you doing home?"

"Lunchtime." He's got a See's sucker in his mouth. He flops onto a big orange pillow with tassels and starts skimming through one of the books. I got the pillows from a school production of *The King and I,* joint effort of St. Michael's and St. Theresa's. They're in the same block, St. Terry's being right next door to my mansion in the Heights. Actually the place belongs to Putz's father, but I did him a favor once and he lets me live in his maintenance garage. He can spare it, he's got two more.

It's eleven o'clock, too early for lunch. Putz has cut out of school again. His dad will beat the crap out of him if he finds out. "Don't bend back the cover, that's an investment," I tell him.

"Hey Jack, you ever run away from home?"

"All the time. On a weekly basis. Used to keep a bag packed expressly for that purpose. Actually it was a handkerchief tied to a stick. That's how Swee'pea did it in *Popeye.* I was a very impressionable young man."

"Don't bullshit me, Jack."

"Yeah, a few times. But you won't get far in that uniform. St. Michael's has a laser dog who's programmed for exactly that kind of plaid. Crrrzzzzz."

"No shit, Jack, sometimes I feel like just taking off. Go out and get a job like you, drive a taxicab. Be my own man."

"I don't drive a taxicab."

"You know what I mean."

"I don't even have a job. What am I, crazy?" I do a mad scientist's laugh, slip in a cassette from the Mucus Men and

12

toss him Mickey Mouse From The Grave. He knows exactly how to turn it on. It's that kid telepathy you lose at around age thirteen. Must have something to do with hormones.

The creature starts bleating out "Saints." Makes an interesting duet with the Mucus Men.

"Bitchen," says Putz. Where he gets the lingo, I don't know. "You just buy this?"

"It was a freebie." I look in the mirror and tousle my dark curly hair for that boyish look. Then I pick up the phone and call my girlfriend Gina.

Her machine clicks on. "Hi, you've reached Gina Matrigali Studios, leave a message, we'll get back to you." *Beep.*

"Gina, it's Jack, just calling to—"

"Jack, you asshole."

"Gina! The real you."

"Fuck you, Jack, what do you want?"

It's all words with Gina. When I'm around she treats me like a king.

"Gina, I want to see you. Come over tonight."

"What the hell for?"

"To be with me. To slither and swoon. To make kissy-kissy."

"Excuse me while I throw up."

"To do the mambo and the funky chicken. Come on, Gina."

"You are so full of shit."

"Gina."

"It just so happens I'm doing my nails tonight."

"Me too. Come over, Gina. Eleven o'clock."

"Why am I talking to you? I should be out shooting today."

"Gina Gina Gina."

"And so articulate. How do women resist?"

"See you tonight, then?"

"Go fuck yourself."

She hangs up. It's a date. Carefully I remove the suit, line up the creases and drape it over a wooden hanger. Then I put on some jeans which I washed just four days ago, and the orange-and-green Hawaiian shirt with little surfers hiding in the leaves. I top it all off with my bright yellow Local Motion cap and prepare to sally forth for lunch.

It's shaping up to be an almost perfect day.

Three

I WATCH THE SUN DROP DOWN from inside the Bilge, a waterfront dive not far from Pier Street where they serve Anchor Wheat on tap. It's decorated with old license plates which are supposed to have come from the junkyard. I happen to know they didn't.

It's a pretty sunset, streaks of pink and gray like a fat coho salmon. Maury the Mariner taps another draft and slides it over in a pool of foam. He's tall and skinny with skin like jerky. He's constantly whistling but you can never make out the tune. After a while you stop hearing it.

I'm the only one who calls him Maury the Mariner. For all I know, he's never been to sea.

"What's! up! Jack!" Maury speaks one syllable at a time. I think it's a respiratory problem.

"Not a whole lot. Keeping busy. Seen Milo tonight?"

"Left! a! note!" He slaps a scrap of paper on the bar. "Be! in! later!"

I nod and ignore the note. Milo knows I can't read his writing. I go to work on the beer, wait another thirty minutes after dark before settling my tab. As the poet once said, I live my life with deliberate speed.

"See you, Maury."

"Right! Jack!"

I drive on down to Jerry Mack's neighborhood. I've got the keys to his truck so there's no need to stop and chat. Tomorrow I'll buy him a ginger ale at the Bilge.

I park behind the truck and remove the license plates. I love riding high, looking down into the other cars. There's something about being able to see people's legs. Once I was at this luncheon on trade with Yap or someplace like that, and the cloth fell away from the front of the speakers' rostrum. All those experts with their legs showing. It was tough taking them seriously.

I need a few minutes to get used to the truck. It's been a while since I've driven one. Okay, so I've never driven one. How hard can it be? Just a few more gears than your average stick. I search for an owner's manual but all I find are porno magazines and motivational cassettes. After a little grinding—Jerry's fault, he left it in gear—I get the engine started. It's noisy as hell. Lucky there'll be nobody on Pier Street this time of night.

I throw the truck into gear and it takes off down the street. I'm bouncing up and down like a paint can in the automatic mixer at Standard Brands. I'm tempted to sound the air horn but I know how upset Jerry would get. He has to live in this neighborhood.

I rumble along toward Pier Street at a steady thirty miles per hour. For some reason I can't shift into the higher gears. Doesn't matter, I think. I need torque, not speed.

Three blocks to go and the area's less deserted than I'd hoped. People are strolling around like tourists at the Wharf. I pull over and kill the engine. After a few minutes of breathing exercises I get out of the truck. I'm just around the corner from the green container. Casually I start walking.

The night is damp and clear, windbreaker weather. Now

I'm in the same block and there's no one in sight, just long, low warehouses with truck bays and junkyards crammed with machinery. I stand next to the container and listen. I wander over to the nearest warehouse. Not a sound from inside.

What the hell. I go back and get the truck.

Only one problem—I can't find reverse. Passenger cars have those little diagrams on the knob of the stick shift. Apparently truck drivers are just supposed to know. Like they're part of some cult.

I work the gears, grinding in every direction. It's like a damn pinball machine, tilt tilt tilt. Outside it's cold but I'm starting to sweat. Why don't I just put up a neon sign? LARCENY IN PROGRESS. All of a sudden the stick finds its groove and the truck lurches backward. Victory!

I maneuver into position and cut the engine. Mistake number one. I start hitching the container to the truck. The chains are noisy and I do a sloppy job but I don't care. It takes about twenty minutes. I'm checking the chains one last time when a man comes out of the shadows.

I swing up into the truck and slam the door. The man is walking toward me. He's a big burly guy in jeans and a dark blue windbreaker. I hit the lock with my elbow and flood the engine. He's two feet away, big and burly. He says, "Hey, you!" I fire up the truck and find second gear from a dead stop, it'll have to do. He's banging on the door now. He's telling me to open up.

The truck shudders and starts to roll. The man slaps a wallet with badge against the window. I look straight ahead and don't stop. The wallet slips away and is replaced by a face. He's climbed onto the running board and is hanging onto my rearview mirror.

I'm up to twelve miles an hour, punishing speed. The man pounds on my window and yanks at the door. I'm whistling "Flight of the Bumblebee" and pretending not to see him.

17

He has a round face and a bushy mustache. I don't make him out to be a city cop, they don't work alone. Maybe a cowboy from DEA. Which means I'm hauling a container full of crack or something. Oh joy.

My neck and hairline are prickly with sweat. I floor the accelerator and coax another two miles an hour out of the truck. I make a sharp left at the corner but the man hangs on. He's still shouting and slamming his fist against the window. His face has a pushed-out look. We're headed east, toward the waterfront. Up ahead is a main street with heavy cross-traffic. The light is red. I finesse the stick shift and find a higher gear.

He yells something like "What the hell are you doing?" We're twenty feet from the intersection and the DON'T WALK sign for the other direction is blinking. My left arm rests on the door, my elbow two inches in front of the lock. My right hand grips the steering wheel. The speedometer edges toward twenty-five.

The light in the other direction turns yellow and we hit the intersection as the man on the running board says "Aw, shit!" I hear the squeal of brakes and the honking of horns. In one smooth move I pull up the lock and throw my shoulder at the door. It flies open and I nearly fall out, saved only by my grip on the steering wheel. I pull back as the man tumbles into the street with a tuck and roll. I ratchet the stick into high gear and the truck lurches ahead, forcing the door shut. The container fishtails, then straightens out. In my rearview mirror I see the man get up and brush off his clothes. Cross-traffic has stopped with room to spare. I turn the corner and he's gone.

My blood is pumping and my head feels light as I drive north. Better than any drug.

I've done a lousy job of hooking up the container, though. There's too much slack in the chain and the chassis keeps running up on the tractor. I slow down and take corners more carefully.

The place I have in mind is five miles away on the northern waterfront, a deserted military bunker on land that's part of a national park. Inside it's pitch black and smells like moldy cement. It's full of things that skitter around and make little clicking sounds with their toenails. Even horny teenagers stay out.

Unfortunately it's at the top of a steep hill with a couple of switchbacks that weren't designed for your average big rig. I'm afraid the container will either break away or pull me back down the hill. I hug the road, being an expert in the low gears by now. The trick is not to stop. At the crest I back the chassis deep into the bunker and cut the engine and lights.

The air goes out of my body with a big *whoosh*. I feel like a kid who just got off the roller coaster and wants to ride it again. My hands are shaking and my brain is doing a speed-metal riff. I do some more breathing exercises, deep and slow.

Dead quiet, nothing to see or hear. This must be what they call an out-of-body experience. I'm floating in pitch-black space, totally free and alone. I sit there for I don't know how long.

Finally I switch on my flashlight and climb out of the truck. The walls are covered with green gray slime and unreadable graffiti. I'm standing in a puddle.

I slosh my way to the back of the container and examine the padlock. It's a nice one. In fact it's a lot nicer than the container, which is banged up in spots and rusting at the corners. The lock could have been bought yesterday.

In my pocket are a couple of shanks. They're metal and U-shaped, they slip down both sides of the shackle into the lock. Then you pull up and Open Sesame. Only the fit on this lock is too snug for the shank. Modern technology.

A couple of picks I carry around get me nowhere. I still haven't replaced my hacksaw. I dispense with subtlety and go for the crowbar. But the shackle's so thick, I can't get any leverage. The crowbar keeps flying loose and threatening to embed itself in my forehead. I try several angles but it's no use. On the last attempt I fall on my ass and get slime all over my pants.

It's late. Jerry needs his truck and Gina will be over to the house soon. I'll have to leave the container and try again tomorrow night.

Maybe I'll bring along some dynamite.

Four

"So, Jack. How's the job going?"

That's my parole officer speaking. Her name is Melanie Robinson and she's what you'd get if your high school boys' vice principal were reincarnated in the body of a beautiful woman. She's five foot ten with a long, straight nose, pale blue eyes, and honey-colored hair which she keeps tied back so people will take her seriously. She doesn't wear any makeup and she scares the hell out of me.

I nod and smile. "Good. Real good."

"Still driving the cab?"

"Oh yeah. Yep. Yes."

"That can be a tough business."

"Tough, yeah. It can be that."

"But you're plugging along?"

"Plugging, yes. Plugging right along."

Melanie nods and looks at me. It's a calm and steady look, as if her eyes had been wandering around the room and just happened to fall on me. But her pupils are like steel pachinko balls.

She glances down at the file. "And you're still living . . ."

"Same place."

"That's a nice neighborhood."

"Oh yeah." Nice is one word for it.

That look again. As if she were patiently waiting for a confession. You can tell me, she's saying, you'll feel so much better . . .

I never cared much for guilt. It's not a big component of the Presbyterian lesson plan. I break off eye contact and look around the office. There's a print from a Van Gogh exhibit over the desk. A Chinese vase of fresh cut flowers. Snapshots of a burly, bearded man in a thick Irish sweater, a couple of kids, and a sheepdog. Also a nice-looking sailboat.

She says, "How's Jerry?"

"Huh?"

"You saw him yesterday."

Meaning she saw him this morning. "Only for a sec," I say. "Just dropped by to see how he was doing."

"Jerry's not as strong as you are, Jack. He gives in more easily to temptation."

I clear my throat.

She says, "He's trying really hard."

I nod.

"Are you?"

"Absolutely. Definitely."

Her stare gets deeper as she decides whether I'm being sarcastic. Then she drops the compassionate act.

"Let me tell you something, Jack. I am not easily bullshitted."

"Yes, Melanie, I know."

"I can't be dicked around."

"Mm."

"You've violated the terms of your parole by seeing Jerry. That I'm willing to let slide. But I have the distinct impression there's something else going on here. And if I'm right,

I'll have you back behind bars so fast you'll swear it was psychic projection. I can do that."

I mull it over for a moment. I'm thinking there are drawbacks to having a beautiful parole officer. It's like having a woman doctor probe your prostate.

"You know," I say, "I once saw this science experiment. There was this rat in a maze. Whenever he made a wrong turn they'd give him a little electric shock. They did this like a hundred times until he learned to go the right way. Even when they put a piece of cheese at the wrong turn, he wouldn't take it anymore. He might sniff at it but he'd keep on going. That's how I see myself today. I may be sniffing the cheese, but I'm not eating it."

She's not looking particularly hostile anymore, but the steel balls are still rattling around. She waits half a minute, then shakes her head. Her voice comes out sad, even a little sympathetic. "I don't know, Jack. I really don't know. You have this penchant for taking the longest shortcut between two points."

The comment doesn't seem to call for an answer so I don't provide one. She closes the file and stands up. "I want to start seeing you every week. And stay away from Jerry."

Maybe you knew me in kindergarten. I was the kid who always got sent to the corner. After about five minutes I'd get up and apologize profusely to the teacher. She would always let me back in the group.

Sometimes I really hate myself.

I have lunch at the Sizzler, which is free because I found a bunch of their all-you-can-eat plates at a restaurant supply house. It's a pretty good salad bar and I've been eating too much red meat lately. Slows me down. After lunch I crank down the windows and cruise around town on a beautiful spring day. There's a saltwater breeze with a touch of kelp. I feel so good I even pick up a couple of fares, happy tourists on their way to the Wharf. I tell them about a great jazz club that doesn't exist. Later I stop at the hardware store to purchase a sledgehammer.

After that, the stationer's store. "Jaaaack," says the old man in tweed behind the counter, as if my name were the answer to the $64,000 Question. He reaches under the shelf and pulls out five blank envelopes: 12 by 15, 10 by 13, 9 by 12, 7 by 10, and letter-sized. And a bag to put them in. I give him exact change. Then he breaks my twenty into 4 fives.

After the post office there's still plenty of time to kill before dark. I drive through a car wash and spend nearly an hour drying and buffing the Checker Marathon. It's built like an armored personnel vehicle but it rusts easily. I got it from a longshoreman in exchange for a metallic green '68 Corvette. No question who got the better part of that deal. Sorry about that bump.

I rub a little too hard and scrape my Bilge decal right off the wind wing. It's a picture of a rat in Ray-Bans lounging in a martini glass with THE BILGE written underneath. I value it highly. This provides me with a reason for returning to the Bilge. The place is more crowded than before, but it's Friday and people are cutting out of work early.

"Jack! what'll! you! have!"

"A draft and a new decal for my cab, Maury. Milo around?"

"Right! over! there!"

I turn just as Milo is coming through the crowd. His white suit stands out like a drive-in movie screen. That plus the fact he's thirty-six inches wide at the shoulders and five feet five inches tall. He shaves his head but he's not going bald, he just likes the way it looks. His body's hard as rock. He looks like a walking picnic cooler, only better dressed.

"I am wondering where you are going, Jack. You are not coming in all night and all day. You are very busy?"

He speaks with an Eastern European accent and his voice

24

sounds strangled. It's not particularly high but it's a *little* voice, you know what I mean? Like a choking squirrel. All comes from not having a neck.

"Not too busy to buy you a Kahlúa and cream, Milo." Pronounced *Mee-lo*. I guide him toward a table. The idea of Milo on a barstool—well, as Nixon's people used to say, it's not operative.

"I am having several interesting pieces to show you," Milo announces. Somehow his voice manages to cut through crowd noise. I gesture to him to shut up until we're sitting down. Milo's a respected antiques dealer on a nice street in Our Fair City. He'd never sell a phony piece to a customer. But he's happy to sell one to me.

"I may have something for you, too," I tell him once we're huddled over a table the size of his head. "But I'm not sure about it yet."

"You are coming over now to *Czech* it out?" he says, enjoying the pun, but I'm not paying attention. Standing at the bar is the burly mustachioed cop who chased my truck, I mean Jerry's truck, the night before. And he's looking right at me.

"Milo," I whisper. "The door!"

Milo bolts up, throws over the tiny table and follows me to the door. He's surprisingly fast. The cop is right behind us. He tries lunging past Milo but he can't reach me. Now I'm outside and Milo is standing in the doorway. Actually he's wedged in the doorway. The cop can't get through because Milo can't budge. It's one of his party tricks.

The cop is swearing and Milo's yelling in Czech and there's all kinds of commotion inside the bar as I jump into the Checker and tear out of the gravel parking lot. The cop's taller than Milo so he probably caught a glimpse of the cab. Maybe he saw it before. I can't figure out how he tracked me down, not until I feel the new Bilge decal in my shirt pocket. Jerry's got one on his truck. This guy is good.

I took off the license plates so they haven't traced the truck. When Jerry gets back from Albuquerque I'll tell him to scrape off the decal. If Melanie Robinson finds out we're both dead. Maybe she already knows. My stomach does a backflip. But she can't know—the cop was waiting for me at the Bilge, not my home. The decal is his only lead.

Plus the knowledge that I drive a cab. And a whole barful of regulars who can identify me. But what could they say? They don't know where I live. Maury the Mariner doesn't even know my last name. And Milo won't talk. He'll say he never saw me before, we were having an argument about religion and he was chasing me out of the bar in anger when he happened to get stuck in the door. Don't you just hate it when that happens?

I stop in an alley and peel off the embossed magnetic door signs which say RAPID CAB. I open the trunk, pull out another set and slap them on. Now I'm MR. TAXI. Then I screw on a new pair of license plates. Afterwards I sit in the car for a while and listen to the Slug Boys. Eventually my heart slows down. That was close, I think. I almost lost it all.

I can't wait for it to get dark.

Five

CLIMBING THAT HILL IN THE CHECKER is a lot easier than in Jerry's truck. I sail right to the top and into the bunker with nobody following. I've tried every trick in the book to flush out a tail. I've even searched the undercarriage for radio tracers, though I don't expect to find any. That's not his style. He's low-tech, a loner, slow and patient. A guy who's seen too many movies.

The container hasn't been touched. I wedge the flashlight into a notch in the back so it's pointing at the ceiling. Then I have another go with the crowbar.

I nearly lose an eye. This is the thickest damned padlock I've ever seen. Finally I bring out the sledgehammer and whale away. It's a direct hit but the lock holds. The echo is deafening.

The sound dies. All's quiet. I put my back into it, smashing at the lock again and again. I'm yelling like a samurai and the sound of the hammer's bouncing off the walls like cannon fire. The air's getting clammy and close. I feel like I'm breaking into an Egyptian tomb only the Pharaohs weren't buried in ocean containers. After a while I stop to catch my breath. My hands are aching. The lock is unharmed.

I swing again. The flashlight slips to the ground and goes out. I grope for it in an inch of greasy water, wedge it more firmly into the back of the container. Once again I heft the sledgehammer, feeling its weight. I take deep breaths and pretend I'm a combination of the Mighty Thor and Ben Grimm, the Thing. It's clobberin' time. Bringing the hammer all the way back I let fly with a bloodcurdling scream. The force of the blow knocks me to the ground. I rise from the slime and inspect the padlock. It hangs open like an overcooked noodle.

Take a breather. I slump against the container and study the ceiling while my muscles recover. My fingers are stiffening up and my palms are starting to blister. I think I tore a rotator cuff. If it's drugs inside I'll call the cops anonymously. If it's toxic waste I'll call EPA. Anything else is fair game. Just for fun I try to imagine what could be worth the trouble.

I push up the retaining rods and the doors creak open. Inside smells like old hay. I shine the flashlight on a wall of cardboard boxes stamped MADE IN HONG KONG. I pull one down, it's light, and tear open the lid. Styrofoam peanuts spill onto the ground. I'm staring at a bunch of faces with ratlike smiles.

I brush away the peanuts to reveal a box full of pudgy rubber dolls. It's a fat, flesh-colored Buddha about eight inches tall, with skinny arms resting on a huge belly and legs in the lotus position. The proportions remind me of Milo. The face is like a cartoon, toothy grin with tiny white teeth. He looks kind of happy and kind of insane. Nirvana. I press my thumbs into his belly and he screams.

It sounds like a small furry animal pinned to the wall with a bayonet. The noise keeps going as I squeeze harder. I let go and the Buddha exhales. The pitch changes slightly but he doesn't stop screaming until his belly returns to its natural shape.

Now there's just the dripping of water and something skittering around in the corner of the bunker. The pudgy little Buddha is grinning at me like I'm the butt of some hilarious joke. I'm thinking I am. I look him over, shake him hard. Nothing rattling around inside. I reach into the carton and come up with more Buddhas and Styrofoam peanuts. I find the same thing in a dozen more boxes.

I switch off the flashlight and sit in the dark on the edge of the container like The Thinker. I think about my chosen vocation. It's not the lack of job security I mind. Something always comes up, like Al Merkel's tip on the green container at the novelty convention. And I like the unpredictability, driving around town in this phony cab looking for opportunities. How many people can wake up in the morning and honestly say they don't know how the day's going to end? Stay loose, you're open to anything that comes along.

The problem is, there's no straight line between effort and results. Once I had a considerable sum of money fall out the back of an armored car. Another time a guy had to beg me to accept a consignment of sterling silver mood rings which I disposed of in fifteen minutes and which netted me a 400-percent profit. Now I spend two days getting chased by a bulldog of a cop, borrow a friend's truck and nearly get us both thrown back in jail, end up covered in slime and sweat, hands all blistered, and I'm the proud owner of a thousand cartons of leering rubber Buddhas with a scream that can pierce your eardrums under laboratory conditions.

Sort of blows the work ethic all to hell.

Six

THERE ARE ANY NUMBER OF WAYS to move spontaneously acquired merchandise but the first place I usually go is Oscar Poole. His rates are competitive and he doesn't dicker. Plus I like his house. He lives in woodlands thirty miles south of the city among architects and heart surgeons and newspaper publishers. From the street you can't see anything but trees and shrubs and mailboxes with numbers, no names. He's discreet.

The house is at the top of a steep gravel drive staked with security patrol signs and guard-dog warnings. The first thing you see driving up is the carport with the Jag and the Lamborghini and the Miata, the Miata belonging to his physical therapist Rowena. Then a series of rough-cut white marble steps wandering up through the prettiest landscaping you can imagine, bright flowers and multicolored gravel and baby pines. The air smells of jasmine. A gurgling stream drops down a series of terraces cut into the hillside, to a crystal-clear pond full of catfish and carp. Pretty strange place for a guy in a wheelchair.

The front of the house is a bunch of white marble cubes

with small square windows and glossy black double doors. The back part is the place to be, a two-story living room in Mediterranean style with one whole wall of glass looking onto a garden like the one where the Eloi hung out in their togas in *The Time Machine* until the Time Traveller came along and screwed things up.

The front doors swing open electronically and Oscar rolls out in his battery-operated wheelchair to greet me personally. Oscar was a rodeo clown, then a Hollywood stuntman. Broke his back trying to retrieve the neighbor kids' softball from a bird's nest in the rain gutter.

"Jack, how you doin'?" Texas accent. Oscar's a little guy, kind of stringy except for his arms, which are built up from working with free weights. Right behind him is Rowena, who could easily bench-press Oscar and probably does.

Oscar backs up and lets me in. Rowena glares at me. She's wearing her usual baggy gray sweat suit with her hair in bangs and the rest of it pulled back in a ponytail. She's six feet tall and outweighs Oscar by at least thirty-five pounds. I make it a point to stay on her good side.

Oscar says, "So what you been up to, Jack? You want a beer or something? Maybe some lemonade?"

"Beer sounds good."

Oscar looks at Rowena, who scowls but goes and gets it. He says, "You like garden statuary, Jack? Greek gods, that kind of thing? I just got me a ton of it."

"Actually I'm selling, not buying."

"Well, spread the word." We pass through the living room and down a cement ramp to the patio, where there's a low stone table with a sweating glass of lemonade and a pitcher with the smiling Kool-Aid face. I pull up a deck chair.

I toss him the plastic shopping bag. "First dibs, Oscar, my man."

"Well, I appreciate that, Jack. You know I do." He opens the bag and pulls out a Buddha. "What in the hell?"

"Press the belly."

He does. Rowena comes charging out, one hand pressing the bulge in the waistband of her sweat suit. Oscar turns to her and laughs. "God*damn,* Rowena! Get a load of this!"

She sighs with disgust, goes back in the house for my beer.

"Jack, you really crack me up."

"I'll crack you up four thousand times over if you'll take the consignment off my hands."

Oscar looks surprised. "This is what you're goin' around sellin'?"

"It's a quality novelty item. Retails for like seventy bucks apiece but I'll take ten. You won't find it in the tourist shops on the Wharf, that's for sure."

Oscar shakes his head, laughs again. "I'd say you're losin' it, Jack, but you've proved me wrong in the past. Anyways it's not my style. Y'all go ahead and try somewhere else. Which is not to say I don't appreciate your comin' here first. Here's that beer."

Rowena comes out with a bottle of Beck's on a reproduction, old-time Coca-Cola tray. "Thanks anyway," I say, "but I've got to be moving along." Rowena puts on a blank expression as I go past her.

"You ever do any freelance total body massage?" I ask her.

"Fuck you," she says.

What is it with certain women and me?

Paco's Ninety-Nine-Cent Bonanza is sort of a moveable feast which pops up in vacant storefronts for several weeks at a time. The landlord makes a few extra bucks and Paco gets another crack at liquidating his inventory of overruns, damaged goods, insurance lots and things nobody in his right mind wants. This spring he's domiciled in a bankrupt furniture showroom out in the avenues. It's a big high room with exposed, corroded pipes and greasy windows. The place is right in front of a bus stop so naturally the front's all covered with graffiti.

Paco's a former Teamster going on sixty with muscles long turned to flab. I doubt he remembers the last time he saw his feet. He chews on an unlit Garcia y Vega as he turns the Buddha over in his big hands.

He says, "You're kidding me, right?"

"I'm a kidder, but I'm not kidding. Come on, Paco, this is like mashed potatoes and gravy for you. It'll practically fly out the door."

"Look around you, Jack. I sell tube socks, hair spray, Cracker Jack in bulk, things people need. I can't move this shit." He shoves the Buddha at my stomach.

"Won't know if you don't try."

"I don't try. Now get the hell out of here. Unless you got some beach equipment. I could really use some beach equipment."

"I came to you first."

"Then you're a lot more desperate than I thought. Now scram."

The Buddha sits on a shaky TV table. He looks disgustingly pleased with himself. Across from me is Al Merkel, the novelty salesman with the homicidal Mickey Mouses. He lives in a top-floor studio apartment at the edge of downtown. The place charges double the going rent just because it has its name on a brass plaque at the entrance: THE ROSEWAY ARMS. I don't see any arms. Just a threadbare runner in the corridor and walls crying for a coat of paint.

Merkel's place is a long, low room with a slanted ceiling and sour-smelling shag carpet. He's got a sofa bed and nightstand at one end, beat-up desk and filing cabinet at the other. All around are boxes full of the thing with the axe which bleats "When the Saints Go Marching In." I'm praying he doesn't turn one on.

Merkel stares at the grinning Buddha. It pays no attention to him. "What am I supposed to do with it?"

"Squeeze it."

He does. It's loud enough to drown out any rendition of "Saints." The belly pops back into place and the Buddha shuts up.

Merkel grunts. "Maybe one box. Swap you for a box of those." He gestures toward the psycho mice.

I shake my head. "Cash only. For the whole consignment."

Merkel rubs his forehead. He's wearing a wilted white dress shirt with sleeves rolled up, and the same pair of gray pants he had on the other day. I want to tell him he needs a better suit.

He squints at me. "I thought you were supposed to be a reporter."

Good memory. "I dabble."

"Where'd you get this crap, anyway?"

"That second container they tried to stick you with."

"Jesus, it was yours?"

I shrug. "Nobody else wanted it."

"Awww." He gives me an irritated look out of the corner of his eye. Then he picks up the Buddha and inspects it with the eye of an expert.

He taps the bottom, where the whistle is. "This could be counterfeit. Buyer could have walked away from the deal when things got hot."

I wonder who'd go to the trouble of counterfeiting something like this. It's not exactly Ninja Turtles.

"Or"—he clutches the Buddha and leans across the TV table—"it could be a sting. A setup by the cops to see who falls into the net. You see anybody out there?"

"No," I say.

He puts the Buddha back on the table, facing me. I feel a chill. His apartment is cold even though we're on the top floor. The building across the street blocks the sun. "Then maybe not," he says. "Or else you lucked out. Anyway I can't use this. I got enough problems as it is."

I thank him and start to leave.

"Hey, you forgot your Buddha."

"Keep it. Payment for the mouse."

He insists. I really don't mind taking it back. I just wish the damned thing would stop grinning.

The little bell over the door jingles as I enter Milo's antique shop. I keep telling him it's a tacky feature, like in a candy store, but he won't listen. I think it reminds him of back home in Czechoslovakia, or whatever the place is called now.

The sign says BY APPOINTMENT ONLY but he keeps the door unlocked. Another example of Old World quaintness. Milo's at the back of the shop talking to a couple in their thirties. The man has a ponytail. He's wearing a pale blue double-breasted suit that's two sizes too large. The jacket has padded shoulders and tapers at the butt like an inverted pyramid. The woman has on a white cotton blazer over a mauve collarless blouse, white pants and those webbed shoes that look cheap but cost a hundred and fifty dollars. I can see her makeup from across the room.

"You're sure about the provenance of this cradle?" the man says.

"Am most certain," Milo says in his squeezed voice. He's wearing his ice-cream suit. "Is most certainly of eighteenth century. Is of that typical Early American style."

"It's so sweet," the woman says.

"Is very sweet," Milo agrees. He has to stand sideways in the aisle to keep from knocking stuff off the shelves.

I've been careful, I parked three blocks away and hid

across the street for twenty minutes before going in. Now I'm lurking behind a shelf of brass curlicues that might be candlesticks, might be napkin holders, might be thumb-screws. It's been a long day and I'm waiting for Milo to accompany me to the Bilge for twenty or thirty stiff drinks. He raises a short-fingered hand to indicate he's seen me. The couple wants to know how many coats of varnish those typical Early Americans put on their cradles. Milo says it depends. They nod solemnly. They're in the presence of an expert.

They go on talking. Next thing they'll ask for breeding papers. Just buy the damned cradle, I want to tell them. It's old and overpriced. What more do you want? I need to talk to Milo.

I'm not going to get the chance. Outside staring through the window is the cop. He's shielding his eyes from the glare. And me behind a glass shelf of brass gewgaws. It's like hiding behind a picket fence.

The bell over the door rings and the cop comes in. I drop to the floor. The woman gives me a puzzled look. I press a finger to my lips and blow her a kiss. The old Squire charm. She looks at her boyfriend/husband. He's too busy talking to Milo to notice. The cop moves into the shop and looks around. He's wearing scuffed brown wingtips, size eleven or twelve. They need new heels.

Milo sees the cop. "You will wait one brief moment," he says. The cops nods and scans the shop at eye level. He's got on a black leather jacket cut like a sport coat, dress shirt open at the collar, creased polyester slacks. He turns in my direction. If he looks down I'm dead.

The woman nudges her companion, who doesn't get the message. Milo clears his throat loudly and draws the cop's attention away from me. No way I can make it to the street. The woman is tugging on the man's coat and whispering in his ear. Milo's trying to guide everyone toward the door.

The man shakes his head and says, "What?" The cop backs toward me to give them room. And I'm thinking that brass isn't breakable.

The cop's directly opposite me when I push the shelf over. It leans against him and rains down brass. One piece falls on his foot and he yells. Those mothers are heavy. The cop is the only thing keeping the shelf from toppling all the rest like dominoes. Milo rushes over to help him out. I squeeze through a gap and make the door. The bell tinkles as I leave.

Antique Row's full of side streets, courtyards, shortcuts. I go in one door, out another, up stairs and down, past a fabric showroom, architect's office, ad agency, Persian rug store going out of business, interior design studio with crappy interior design, mezzanine overlooking an atrium, atrium overlooking an art gallery. At some point I start to giggle. The adrenaline's going to my head. I told you I love this part. At last I find a cobbled pathway which winds around a European-style kiosk and leads out to the street where I parked my cab.

The key's in my hand. I slip it into the lock, bull's-eye. I yank open the door and jump in. Just then a big, brown UPS delivery truck pulls alongside and starts flashing its warning lights. I tap my horn politely. The driver writes on a clipboard. I honk again. Still no response. He disappears into the back of the truck. I get out of the cab, go over and knock on his window. He slides open the door and climbs down with an armful of parcels and the clipboard. We meet around the front of his truck.

"Sign here," he says.

"You're blocking my cab," I say.

"Huh?" He looks around, finally notices the cab. "You want out?"

"Yeah."

"Just be a sec." He starts toward the sidewalk.

"I want out *now*."

"Huh? Oh." He looks like I've set his truck on fire. I will if he doesn't move it. He mutters something and climbs back in the truck. I get into my cab and start the engine. He pulls forward instead of backing up. I'll still have a tough time getting out. I shift into reverse as a hand grabs my shoulder and the cop with the big red face and mustache bobs into my rearview mirror.

"Stop the motor," he says.

Seven

I SAY, "WHERE YOU HEADED?"

The cop grunts. "Out of the car, please."

Up close he's older than I thought, with broken blood vessels in his nose and crinkles around his eyes. I figure he's forty-five, maybe fifty. His temples aren't gray but it might be a dye job. His hair's reddish brown, brushed straight back and breaking over the ears. A gold wedding band is embedded in his finger. He has a middle-age paunch. He's six foot one and two hundred pounds minimum.

He makes me assume the position, hands on the car and legs spread, in full view of the public. Getting arrested is an embarrassment. It makes you feel special in the wrong way. Everybody's free to walk down the street, drive a car, stand around with their jaws hanging open. Everybody but you.

He skips the patdown and goes directly into the spiel. I'm barely listening.

I say, "What?"

He says, "Huh?"

"Let me see that." I'm pointing to the wallet with his badge. He holds it up to my nose. I have to pull back to read it. "You're not a cop."

"Special Agent Bailey, U.S. Customs Service. A cop like any other. And you're busted." He fastens the handcuffs a little too tightly. "That's for being a smartass." It's a trait I'm working on.

He leans into the cab and finds my wallet in the glove box. With one hand he flips it open. "Mr. Squire," he says.

It's not a question. He pockets the wallet and takes me by the arm.

People are starting to gather. Luckily his car is two doors down. It's a gold, unmarked Dodge Dart with rust around the windows and fast-food wrappers on the gold vinyl seats. He puts me in back, which smells like french fries. I get the feeling he's spent a lot of time in this car on stakeout. My opinion of him softens a bit. I vow to be nicer.

There's a police radio up front but he doesn't use it. He's going through the wallet. My picture of Gina falls out onto the seat. I start to say something nice about her but he keeps going. He flips through the bills and several forms of false ID. Finally he starts the car, which responds immediately.

"Good old slant-six engine," I say. "Don't make 'em like that anymore."

He pulls into traffic and works his way east to the docks, then south. We're headed toward the warehouse where I borrowed the green container.

"This area sure has changed a lot," I say.

He doesn't answer. For some reason I feel the need to draw him out.

"Funny isn't it, all these trucks and warehouses and not a ship in sight. Everything's tourists and conventions now, and that's fine for me, I'm a cabbie, but others? The blue-collar workforce? The big factories? That's the heart of a city. Next big recession, you better believe we'll feel it. I'm feeling it now. You notice how dead it seems around town? It's just a sense I have. I don't have any figures to back it up."

I might as well be talking to the Buddha. He just keeps on driving and chewing his wad of gum. Finally he pulls up to an abandoned two-story office building directly across the street from where the green container was parked. Al Merkel was right, I'm thinking, the whole thing was a setup. They were just waiting for some genius to come waltzing into the trap.

He pulls me out of the car and guides me by the arm into the building. I think of a line from an old Jimmy Cagney movie: *Get your hands off me, screw, I know the way!* Only Cagney was going to the electric chair. I wonder where I'm going.

The place looks empty and smells like it hasn't been aired out for a while. Bailey nudges me up crumbling steps dotted with pigeon droppings. Upstairs the sun shines through gaps in the boards and a big hole in the roof. The light is thick with dust. A rusty block and tackle hangs from a beam. The wall on the street side consists of grimy, small-paned windows, a third of which are broken out. In the corner by the windows is a desk made out of a door and cinder blocks.

Bailey dumps his keys and my wallet onto a pile of fast-food wrappings and falls into a creaky chair. He motions for me to sit on a packing crate in front of the desk. The guest chair. My shoulders, which were already sore from batting practice with the sledgehammer, ache like hell.

"Listen," I say. "The handcuffs?"

He nods, comes around with the keys, and removes the cuffs. Another point in his favor. The blood rushes into my hands like lava.

He sits down again. Over his shoulder I can see the roof of the warehouse across the street. Agent Bailey doesn't care about the view, he's seen it enough times. I picture him sitting in front of those windows for hours, days maybe, humming golden oldies and eating Big Macs. Right now he's chewing on the wad of gum and tapping a finger on the desktop like an old-time telegraph operator.

I say, "How long since you quit smoking?"

He's not offended. "Six weeks."

"It starts to get better after about six months. You never completely lose the urge. You think you're clear of it, but one day you'll be at a party where everybody's drinking. And drinks and cigarettes, they just seem to go together. There's something about that."

He nods slowly. "Where's the container?"

"In a bunker at the fort near the bridge."

He's not taking notes, though there could be a tape recorder going. "And the merchandise?"

Some merchandise. "I don't know. The container was empty when I opened it up. It's all a big mix-up."

A little smile forms under his bushy mustache. I smile back.

"Listen," I say, "you think you could get me a set of those trading cards with the dogs that sniff out drugs?" Believe it or not, they're worth money. Some people will collect anything.

He says, "How long you been involved?"

"I told you, I'm not. One day I saw the container just sitting there all alone and I got curious."

"And you just happened to have a truck."

"I stole it." I don't want to get Jerry Mack involved. Melanie Robinson is right, he really is trying.

He shakes his head. "That's bullshit. You work with Rollaway."

"Who?"

He strokes his mustache with stubby fingers. A single bodacious hair is growing in the wrong direction, sticking right up his nostril. I want to grab a scissors and trim it.

"Give me some names."

Now it's a friendly voice, as though he'd like to see me get

42

out of this. On this point we agree. Unfortunately I'm in a double bind. I don't have any names to give, and if I did I wouldn't. Never have, never will.

"Look," he says, still sympathetic. "I know you're just a little guy. Maybe you're some kind of a gofer. Maybe you tune up the trucks. But unless you give me something right here and now, something about your boss, you're going down with the rest of them, I guarantee it."

"Sorry," I say. "There's nothing to give. I work alone." Got to remind Jerry to scrape that Bilge sticker off his window.

Bailey says "Hunh" and reaches under the desk. He brings up a thermos and two insulated paper cups. He raises an eyebrow and I nod.

"It's cold," he apologizes. "Not too fresh."

"That's okay. I like it aged."

Aged it is. Like several stakeouts old. Tastes fine to me.

In midsip I notice the pictures. They're in two little hinged gold frames on the edge of the desk.

"You mind?" I ask him.

He hands them over. A middle-aged woman, bit on the heavy side, still attractive. A blond girl of eleven or twelve and a brown-haired boy around seven. Everybody smiling.

"Nice," I say. "Does the Customs Service know you're here?"

Bailey looks surprised. I've been adding it up: no call to headquarters after the arrest, no phone on the desk, no sign of a partner, the family pictures. His own little private office.

He says, "What the hell difference does it make to you?"

"Don't get huffy. I'm just thinking maybe you work alone, too. Plenty of people are no good in groups."

"I'm an official agent of the U.S. Customs Service. I'm just off-budget is all. Things are a little tight right now."

I put up a hand. "It's fine, really. No disrespect intended."

He's already forgiven me. Now he makes a big deal out of spreading the handcuffs in the center of the desk. They look like Poindexter's spectacles from the old *Felix the Cat* cartoons. "Suppose you tell me all about it, Mr. Squire."

Uncle. "I found a container full of rubber Buddhas that scream bloody murder when you squeeze their bellies. I was hoping to dump 'em on some discount chain, but the whole thing's turned out to be more trouble than it's worth. My cab is really a front for a wide variety of unscrupulous but ultimately penny-ante schemes. I live in the maintenance garage of an eccentric millionaire in the Heights who hates his kid. My girlfriend swears like a sailor. I've never smoked a cigarette in my life."

He folds his hands across his paunch and leans back in the creaky chair. He looks proud of himself. I don't know what else to tell him.

I say, "It was a good run, wasn't it?"

He says "Hunh" and sips the cold coffee. Something in his eye tells me he thinks so, too. I like most cops, especially the good ones.

His body is beginning to sag, like a snowman just before the thaw. He looks tired. I'm disappointing him and I feel bad about it.

He says, "How old are you?"

"Thirty-one. I'm sorry I left that out."

"For some reason I thought younger."

"Lots of people make that mistake. My girlfriend says I ought to get a job. How about you?"

"Forty-eight."

"No kidding? You must be close to having your twenty years in."

"Pretty close."

"Yeah? What's your wife think about it? She want you to retire?"

"I like the work," he says.

"I can tell. You're good at it."

"Don't bullshit me now."

"I'm not bullshitting you, Bailey, I mean it. You tracked me down without a hell of a lot to go on. I'm impressed."

The little smile under the mustache is frozen, like a constipated walrus. He's doing his best to hide it. The man must not get a lot of support from headquarters, judging from this crummy little setup. They probably give him a hard time about his expense account. Shitload of red tape over a few Big Macs.

"My wife doesn't mind," he says. Doesn't want to let the subject drop. Sitting up here for days on end, he's got nobody to talk to.

"Hardest thing about being a cop," I say, "is not getting support from the family. You're lucky there."

He gives a little laugh. "You been married?"

"Me? Unh-unh. Nope. Maybe one of these days. My girlfriend brings it up a lot. Subtly."

"It ain't so bad. Something to come home to at night."

"Yeah, but you lose a certain amount of flexibility. Guess I'm not ready for that."

Bailey's looking at the handcuffs as if they might have something to say on the subject. At last he heaves a big sigh and stands up. "We're not finished here," he says in a tired voice, then handcuffs my wrists behind my back to the packing crate, which turns out to be nailed to the floor. He pockets the keys. And here I thought we were making progress.

He disappears from view. It's not easy turning around so I stare at the empty office chair and listen for clues about what's going on behind my back. I wonder how long I'll be there. My shoulders are beginning to ache again.

Which is nothing compared with the pain from the blow to the back of my skull. It rattles my eyeballs and smashes my forehead into the edge of the desk. I have a split second to register how badly it hurts before blacking out.

I wake up in the same position, slumped against the desk with my wrists still cuffed to the crate. My head feels stuck in a metal stamping machine and my arms are like bungee cords in a tractor pull. I can taste blood in my nostrils but there's none on the desk. I must have one hell of a bruise, probably a concussion on top of it. Maybe I was kicked by a steel-toed boot.

I try sitting up and am immediately dizzy. Only then does it occur to me that if I move, I might get hit again. I put my head down but that only makes it throb. No position is a good position. I sit up straight and steel myself for another blow.

None comes. Nor any voices. I try thinking about what to tell Agent Bailey when he comes back. Because I'm reasonably certain now that he's not in the room. The son of a bitch is making me sweat. Damned U.S. Customs agents. I didn't know they were so tough.

After a couple of minutes I risk turning around. It seems I was wrong. Agent Bailey is in the room after all. He's three feet off the floor, hanging from a hook at the end of the block and tackle. The hook enters his body just beneath the rib cage. Blood is dripping onto the pigeon shit below.

I scream like the fucking Buddha.

Eight

OKAY, HERE WE ARE. That'll be nine dollars and fifteen cents. Make it nine even. I hate change.

What happened after that? A lot more happened after that. But I'm double-parked, you know?

You really want to know? Drive around awhile, hear the rest?

Suit yourself. That's another big plus to what I do. Flexible hours.

I stop screaming. I hear my own breathing, pigeons' flutter and coo, creak of the block and tackle. And a soft ripping sound, the hook working its way through his ribs. I try standing but I've forgotten about the handcuffs. My tailbone slams into the crate and I feel a stabbing pain in my arms and neck. I scream again. Why not just put it on the PA system? Hey, fellas! I'm still alive, come back and finish me off! Have to admit, I wasn't thinking clearly. Neither would you.

Still no footsteps, nobody coming. I yank at the cuffs. The crate is nailed down good. I try again but the slat barely gives. The problem is getting enough force into it with my

47

hands behind my back. Now I can hear a siren in the distance. I sit for a moment and collect my thoughts, such as they are.

It's all mental, I think. Everything's mental. I'm just going to stand up, ignore the crate, move right through it. That's how karate masters break bricks with their bare hands. I unwind with a rebel yell and stand up—well, almost. Actually I land right back on my butt. But the crate has budged a little, there's a bent nail sticking halfway out of the floor. I do it again, never mind the pain. I hear the cracking of wood. On the fifth try something snaps and I go plowing into the desk. It hurts.

I stand up with about half the crate hanging off my arms. I smash it against the desk but it still won't come off. Because of the crate I can't get my legs through the chain. Meanwhile the body of Agent Bailey twists slowly toward me as the siren comes closer. I'll have to take the crate with me. Then I think: key.

It's in his pocket. I kick another crate into position, step onto it, turn my back to the body, and feel for his jacket pocket. I can do this. But it's going to take two crates. I stack another and step up.

I take a second to find my balance. That Zen thing again. Slowly I reach back and touch his jacket. He bumps against me. My fingers feel leather and find the pocket lip. I probe around, twist my wrists to get in deep where the keys are. Fingertips brush metal. I'm trying to hook the ring when something flies into my face. It's a pigeon out of the rafters like a Japanese Zero. I lose my balance and the crates give way. My hand gets caught in the pocket and the body comes crashing down on top of me.

I heave it off and roll clear. I think I dislocated my shoulder. The good part is that the crate fragment has broken away from the handcuffs. I scramble back to the body and grope for the pocket. I have to roll him over to find it.

Finally I get hold of the keys. Thirty seconds later the cuffs are in my pocket and I'm headed for the door. The siren's about a block away. At the last moment I rush back into the room and grab Agent Bailey's family pictures off the desk.

I soak for two hours in the old claw-foot bathtub from one of the Huffingtons' nine bathrooms. When they remodeled they gave it to me. It takes twenty-five minutes to fill and barely fits in my bathroom, which used to be a utility closet, then a toilet for the house mechanic. I have to stand in the bathtub to reach the mirror and shave. One reason why I don't shave every day.

I hurt all over. My wrists are pretty badly scraped up and my shoulder throbs like a suction pump. My girlfriend Gina will tell you that I have a very low tolerance for pain.

I sit in hot water up to my chin and stare at the pictures of Agent Bailey's wife and kids. She's in a garden full of flowers and wearing a bulky knit sweater with her hair messed up like she's been planting tulip bulbs. The boy and girl are standing on a sidewalk in church clothes and squinting into the sun.

The glass is steaming up so I close my eyes and still I see the Bailey family in their brass-plated frames from the five-and-dime. My skin's getting pruney and the pain's not so bad anymore. Maybe my shoulder's not dislocated after all. I towel off and put the pictures on the shelf beside my own collection of dime-store frames over the futon. The only difference is, I keep the pictures they come with. They look like singing stars from the Frankie Bobby Connie era. I tell Putz they're my mom and dad.

I fold my bloodstained clothes and put them away in one of Gina's photographic-paper boxes. Then I call the police. That siren I heard went right by the warehouse without stopping. I dial the regular number instead of 911 so they can't trace the call.

"Police department."

"There's a dead guy in an old building over on . . ." I give the address. "His name is Special Agent Bailey and he works for the U.S. Customs Service."

A beep on the line. They're recording it. "Sir? Would you state your name and address, please?"

"Just get the guy who did it, all right?" He had a wife who gardens and kids who go to Sunday school. I repeat the address and hang up.

I start looking for some clean clothes. I feel an urge to get out of the house. I dig around for my wallet to check the cash situation.

My wallet's gone. I think I must have left it in the cab, or maybe it fell out at Gina's. It's not that big a deal because I have plenty of false IDs. Then my stomach goes cold. My wallet is at the warehouse.

Agent Bailey had it. He put it right there in front of me on the desk. I try to remember if it was still there when I came to. But I can't picture the room in my mind, all I can see is his body hanging from a hook. Meanwhile I'm thrashing all over the place for some clothes. I put something on, don't bother with socks, don't even tie my shoes. Maybe there's time.

I drive like a maniac. Nobody cares, it's a cab. I keep thinking the cops will take their time, be in the middle of a shift change, think it's a prank call. Odds are I'll make it.

I'm behind one of those big sedans going five miles under the speed limit on a narrow street. The driver's wearing a fedora. Ever notice that the people who drive too slow are the ones who run all the stop signs? I cut over and go the wrong way down a one-way street for a block. I come back around just as the guy in the sedan is sailing through the intersection. I'm still behind him and he's slowing down.

I go for the siren. It's a little thing I had built into the grille. I hate using it because it attracts attention, but I'm desperate. I flick this switch under the dash and give him a couple of seconds of pandemonium. The guy in the sedan jerks to a stop and I almost rear-end him. He's looking all around, like Where's the cop/ambulance/firetruck? I get past him and floor it.

I make it down to the warehouse district in twelve minutes flat, not bad for going from north to south, considering that all the fast streets in Our Fair City run east-west. Anyway I come around the corner and run smack into a herd of cop cars parked at crazy angles outside the warehouse. A uniform directing traffic signals for me to turn around and go back. Joe Citizen obeys and drives away.

Nine

AND KEEPS ON DRIVING. Swearing all the way. I've left my wallet in some bad places but this is ridiculous. Soon as the cops trace my P O box they'll be knocking at my door. This is ungood.

I stop at a phone booth and call Putz. He's got a private phone in his bedroom.

"Yeah."

"Putz."

"Yeah."

"Jack. Listen, man, any cops come around?"

"Haven't seen you. Don't know you. Never heard of you."

"Not now, Putz. I'm just asking if you've seen any."

"Hold on, man, let me look."

Pause on the line.

"Shit, Jack, it's SWAT-team city, they've got the whole fucking block cordoned off, it's the National Guard!"

"Come on, Putz."

"Sorry. Ain't nobody I can see."

"Isn't anybody. They show up, you know what to do.

Meanwhile listen, get downstairs and gather up a change of clothes and my toothbrush. Then wait for further instructions."

"Aye, aye, Capitano."

I drive over to Gina's place. She lives on the fourth floor of a condo conversion in an alley just a few blocks up from Chinatown. You can sit on her deck on a summer afternoon, drink a beer and watch the fog creep over the hills and into the bay. Sometimes we'll barbeque a couple of steaks, one at a time, because that's all her little Hibachi can take. Everything in Gina's apartment is designed for one: one bedroom, one chair, one frying pan. Personally I think she takes it too far.

She buzzes me up. She's waiting on the landing outside her door. Gina always comes out to meet me.

I hand her a dozen long-stem roses. I get a 40-percent discount from my phony dealer's pass at the Flower Mart.

She takes the flowers and gives me a kiss. Holding a little something back. I can tell the flowers are making her suspicious. I say, "Listen, I may need to stay over here a few days."

"You get kicked out on the street again? What's it this time, you burn down the mansion for the insurance?"

"It's nothing like that. I'm just pining for a little domestic bliss."

She takes a deep breath of roses. "So get yourself a fucking wife." Gina gives mixed messages. Her therapist tells her it's self-defense but I don't know against what.

"I'll wash the dish." I follow her into the apartment. "Come on, Gina, I'm desperate here. I need a place to stay. Purely temporary."

She reaches under the kitchen sink and brings out her vase. "That's a relief," she says. "I'd hate to think you were contemplating anything permanent."

This is a sensitive subject and I don't bite. Anyway Gina

53

is busy arranging the flowers on the bar. She doesn't seem too upset.

I put my arms around her from behind. She flinches, then relaxes. I bury my nose in her thick dark hair, which smells like creme rinse. Better than flowers.

"We should eat something," she says, then turns to face me. I give her a long, deep kiss. Eventually she gives it back. It always takes Gina a few minutes to warm up, like somebody's been talking to her during the time we were apart. Eventually she even cuts out the swearing.

The apartment is small so it's a short trip to the bedroom. A single bed, of course. After a while Gina brings out the scarves and ties me to the bedpost. Her therapist would probably say it's that self-defense thing again, like I'm King Kong and have to be restrained. I figure it's harmless enough so I let her do it.

At 2 A.M. Gina is fast asleep against me and I'm staring at the ceiling. The projector in my head is playing out pictures of Agent Bailey, his family, and thousands of big fat laughing Buddhas. Also the cops battering down the Huffington's garage door.

I wonder how long I can last on the streets. They won't be looking for a cab. There's nothing in my wallet to identify me as a cabdriver and Agent Bailey kept to himself. He was a lone wolf, probably didn't even take notes. One hopes.

My stomach goes cold. Gina's picture is in my wallet. I took it one day when she wasn't looking. She's one of those photographers who hates having her picture taken. We were on the beach for a photo shoot and her long black hair was blowing around like a shampoo commercial. I had to run like hell to protect the film. Later on she slipped it into my wallet.

I can't go to Milo's, I was seen with him. Or the Bilge either, even though Maury the Mariner's got a cot in back that I use from time to time. The way I see it, Agent Bailey has pretty much roped off my life. You can't help respecting the man. Guy like that deserves more than to have me arrested for his murder.

Anyway, I can't stay here. I think about sneaking into a room at one of the big downtown hotels—I've got copies of six or seven room keys—but decide it's not worth the risk. I'm going to stay pure for Agent Bailey. Let the Buddhas rot.

I gather up my clothes in the dark and get dressed in the living room. On my way out the latch shuts behind me with a loud click. I put my shoes on at the bottom of the stairs.

I drive over to the big industrial-orange bridge that spans the mouth of the bay like the entrance to a theme park. I leave the Checker in the south lot and stroll out to the walkway. It's a nice time to be out. You can see all the lights of the other people who are up, too. At midspan I casually reach into my pocket and toss Agent Bailey's handcuffs over the side. Man, I wish I hadn't done that.

Later I find an empty carport on a quiet side street and spend the rest of the night in my cab. I don't have any dreams that I can remember.

Next morning I call Putz before he goes to school. No cops have shown up yet. I have him meet me around the corner from St. Michael's with deodorant and clean clothes. Then I shower at the Press Club, where the morning guy knows me and thinks I'm a member.

It's another bright and sunny day but I could really use a cup of coffee. I don't sleep well in cars. I stop at a downtown doughnut shop and slide into a bright orange plastic booth with a twelve-ounce java, eighteen doughnut holes and the morning paper.

Agent Bailey's murder has made the front page. GRISLY SLAYING OF CUSTOMS CLERK. SEE BELOW. That's not nice, I think, calling him a "clerk." No respect for the civil service.

55

> The body of a data processing clerk with the
> U.S. Customs Service was found in a vacant
> office building on Pier Street yesterday, vic-
> tim of what police believe is a drug-related
> murder.
>
> Raymond Bailey, 48, was found at 225
> Pier Street with a grappling hook in his ribs.
> Police were summoned to the scene by an
> anonymous tip. The cause of death was not
> disclosed.

"Try grappling hook," I say aloud.

> The victim was employed by U.S. Customs
> as an input clerk, responsible for entering
> data into the agency's computer . . .

"That's not right," I say. The people at the counter glance
over at me, then look away. I read on.

> "Could have been a drug deal gone sour,"
> said Homicide Inspector Bernard Lutz. "Vic-
> tim could have been the inside man."

"He was a cop, you idiot," I say. Smearing the reputation
of U.S. Customs Special Agent Ray Bailey, one tough and
honest cop. What will his wife and kids think?

> A spokesman for Customs said Bailey had
> access to detailed information about in-
> coming shipments . . .

"Give me a break," I say.

"Hey, mister," the man in the next booth says. He's
wearing a stocking cap and a dirty denim jacket. His face is
caked with grime and his front teeth are missing. "Keep that
shit to yourself."

"Not a chance," I say, downing the last doughnut hole.

* * *

See, here's the thing. Most cops are just doing their job. A few are better than that. Guys like Agent Bailey, tough old bulldogs who'll run you to ground no matter what. You've got to respect that kind of professionalism.

I see it as a game with rules: I run, you catch. Which is more than half the fun. What kind of a world would it be, if we could go around doing whatever the hell we wanted?

Now along comes somebody who breaks those rules, busts on in and hangs up Agent Bailey by a hook. This is when I get pissed off. Add to that he's a family man, wrongly accused of dealing dope, and he doesn't even get to be a cop in the papers. The man deserves somebody on his side. The man deserves an avenger in a yellow cab.

Al Merkel answers the door in a ratty terry-cloth robe and drawstring pajama bottoms with a repeating pattern of little clocks. He doesn't recognize me even though it's only been a day since last we met. Chalk it up to the early hour.

He sees the Buddha in my hand and groans. "Aw, hell," he says.

"Don't worry, Al, I'm not selling. Got any coffee?"

The boxes full of Psycho Mickeys are nicely stacked. Al Merkel rubs his forehead and sits on the unmade bed. Ixnay on the coffee, which is fine with me. His gray suit hangs in dry-cleaner's plastic on the handle of the filing cabinet. He looks at me hopefully. "You change your mind about the consignment?"

"Strike two, Al. I'm not here to do business. Just to ask about this." I put the Buddha on the TV table, whip it around to face him.

Merkel winces. "For God's sake don't make it scream." He's not a morning person.

"Take it easy. I'm only here to talk." I pull up a card chair. "Tell me about this . . . thing."

"What do I know about it?"

57

"Calm down, Al. I'm just picking your brain. What's it take to bring something like this into the country? What's it all about? Tell me the whole story."

"Doesn't take a lot." Merkel's perking up. "Buyer, seller, letter of credit maybe, purchase order, bill of lading, freight bill. Broker takes care of most of that."

"How would you go about forgetting you ordered something? How's something like this end up on the street?"

"Maybe nobody ordered it. Could be a mistake at the seller's end. Some glitch somewhere, anything can happen, usually does."

Not good enough. "Yeah, but how? How's it slip through all those people? How's it get past Customs?" My experience is nothing gets past Customs. Somebody ought to do a reality-based television show about those guys.

Merkel screws up his face like Psycho Mickey. "Could be part of a larger consignment. Got split off from the rest."

"And stuck onto your order. You sure you didn't order it?"

He shakes his head, stands up, pulls a piece of paper out of the nightstand. It's the same one he waved in my face at the toy show. "See for yourself. Two hundred cartons of . . . whatever the hell you call them." Merkel looks really depressed. I'm glad I'm not him.

I take the paper and look it over. The back is still sticky with bubblegum. There's nothing on it about rubber Buddhas. All along I've been thinking it was a sting of Agent Bailey's, but if it was, how did the container get to Al Merkel? I give him my sternest look, straight in the eye. "Al? Are you mixed up in something shady?"

He gets indignant. His body starts to tremble and he spits out the words. "Nobody never . . . I never . . . I'm an honest businessman."

I want to say that's his problem. "Listen, you got a knife around here?"

"A what?"

"Like a steak or carving knife. Preferably a sharp one."

There's a weird look on his face but he goes over to the kitchenette in the corner and opens a metal drawer. He roots around in the utensils and pulls out a long serrated carving knife with a black plastic handle.

"That's perfect," I say.

He hands it to me point first. Obviously the man was never a Boy Scout. "What are you going to do?" he asks.

I pull the rickety TV tray toward me and lay the Buddha on his back. I hold the knife high and plunge it deep into his big rubber belly. Merkel backs up against the file cabinet. He looks horrified as I saw open the Buddha from navel to throat. I drop the knife, jam my thumbs into the slit, and pull him apart.

He's totally hollow and smells like rubber. At least he's not screaming anymore. Merkel gets up enough courage to come over. He looks at the Buddha as if it's going to jump off the table and eat his face.

"Al? Let me see that piece of paper again." He holds it out with a shaky hand. "What was that you were saying about a broker? What kind of a broker?"

"Customs broker. Takes care of the paperwork, clears the shipment, that kind of thing."

"You said before it was the broker who screwed up the paperwork. You mean he cleared these Buddhas, too?"

"Hell, I assume so."

"You mention anything about this to him?"

A nervous shake of the head. "Haven't had the time. Been busy figuring out a way to unload this other crap."

The name of the broker is on the sheet of paper. Ingmar Morgenstern & Co., Inc. With offices right here in Our Fair City.

"Tell you what, Al. Why not let me handle it? Save you all that time and trouble. Keep you totally uninvolved."

He tightens his robe and shrugs. "Suit yourself."

I stop at the door. "Al."

"Huh."

"Insure the Psycho Mickeys to the max. Then dump the whole lot of them into the bay. That's what I'd do."

He looks confused. I leave him to mull over my free advice. I figure I owe him something.

Ten

ON MY WAY OVER TO THE CUSTOMS broker's office I sketch
out a plausible story. I'll be a millionaire importer who got
the Buddhas by mistake, I'm curious to know who ordered
them, they're so damned unique. Tell me and I'll throw
some business your way. Either that or I'm a U.S. Customs
agent investigating a Taiwanese counterfeiting ring. You
never want to overplan, it sounds phony. Anyway I'm best
on my feet.

Ingmar Morgenstern & Co., Inc. is down by the airport
in a one-story prefab which it shares with a wholesale swim-
ming-pool supply house. There's a chain-link fence all
around the property and a metal plaque with the name of a
security service. The gate is chained open and looks like it's
never been closed. Along one side of the building is a row
of plastic signs in front of each parking space: INGMAR,
BETTY, ZOLTAN, NIGEL. Or something like that. I park the
cab out of sight because it doesn't befit a successful importer
with a taste for quality.

A 747 goes roaring overhead. They must get used to it. I
shove a box of Buddhas under my arm and go inside.

On the left is a high counter with the day's mail wrapped in a rubber band, next to a wooden message box with slots for everybody. Behind the counter is a phone system with all kinds of buttons and a computer screen on a retractable arm. There's no one at the desk and the phone is ringing like crazy.

"Somebody!" yells a woman who flies by me like I'm invisible. She's lugging an armful of books and files and moves like a truckstop waitress at high noon. Five or six others are in the room and they're all acting the same way.

The place is one big room with old-style venetian blinds, half a dozen desks facing the same direction, file cabinets which don't match, computers which do. The walls are cheap paneling and covered with travel posters stuck up with thumbtacks. One door in the back is closed and the other leads into a corridor. A jumbo jet flies over and the whole place rattles.

A skinny woman with her hair imprisoned by barrettes dives for the phone. She's so out of breath she can scarcely get out the company's name. Meanwhile a guy in his early twenties dumps a huge computer printout on the desk beside me and starts rifling through it in semidesperation. His hair is thick on top and shaved on the sides, with a little tail at the nape. It looks like a big black sea sponge taking a ride on his scalp.

Finally the first woman sees me. "What now what now what now," she mutters, and motions for me to put down the box. "Wait," she says. "Just wait one minute. You want me to sign something? Just one sec. I know it's here." There's a touch of German in her voice, a singsong tone and trouble with the *w*s. "Goddamn *fucking* computers."

She starts touching stacks of paper on a desk like a mentalist on speed. She's in her mid-thirties, blond and big-boned, but she isn't fat. Wearing a turtleneck sweater with an oversized collar and a tight skirt that quits a couple inches above the knee.

The skinny woman with the barrettes hangs up the phone and calls out to the blonde: "That was Carlos, Sigi. He's stuck on a repair job in the Valley and won't be able to make it over today."

Sigi growls like a bobcat and swings around with an envelope in her hand. "Typical!" she says, then freezes. She's staring at my box. The flaps are open and she sees a layer of the grinning Buddhas. She looks from them to me and back again. "Okay," she says, as if she's reassuring herself that everything is. "Okay, goddamn it."

She puts down the envelope and points toward the acoustic ceiling. "Just a minute," she says and starts walking away. Then she turns and looks at me.

She says, "What happened to Michael?"

"Huh?"

She does a never-mind shake of the head. Then she goes to the closed door at the back and knocks. Everyone stops moving.

A voice from inside, muffled. Sigi timidly opens the door, goes in, closes it behind her. I stand there watched by everybody. The phone's ringing but nobody bothers to pick it up. A minute goes by. Anything to break the ice. "Hey look," I say. I take out a Buddha and squeeze its belly.

"Jesus!" yells the guy with the tail. The skinny woman acts scared. An older man with half-glasses and a cardigan sweater looks at me like Who let *you* in? "Breaks the ice at parties," I say.

After a minute or so Sigi comes out of the office. She stands beside the open door and motions me over. I pick up my box o' Buddhas and go in to see the big cheese.

The guy behind the desk looks tall even sitting down. He's blond going gray, with skin that looks overexposed to the frozen tundra or whatever it is they have in Scandinavia. He wears a dark gray undertaker's suit and a white shirt with a collar that's a couple sizes too big, assuming they make a size for that neck. He has a very prominent Adam's apple. He looks like a place to hang the suit.

"Sit down," he says with an accent I take to be Danish. Goddamn United Nations right here at Ingmar Morgenstern & Co., Inc. He looks past me. "Sigi." She's standing at the door.

Ingmar looks back at me. "Coffee? Tea?"

"Coffee black."

He trades another look with Sigi, who looks pissed to be playing secretary. But she goes out and closes the door.

Ingmar sits back stiffly as if life after death doesn't favor lubrication of the joints. His office has the same bad paneling but a nicer carpet, a three-month calendar from Evergreen Lines and a big walnut trophy case along one wall. Inside it are shiny plaques, pictures of Ingmar shaking hands with people, team photos with guys in white pants.

"Well," he says. "That was extremely fortunate."

"I'll say it was." Like I'm saying, fortunate for you. I'm following his lead.

"It just got lost in the *shuffle*?" His voice goes up on the last word. He gives a little smile, like he's proud of his ability to speak slang.

I nod gravely. "Shouldn't have happened, though."

He swallows. "No, of course not." He tries another smile. "You must excuse us today, the computers . . ." He waves a hand as if to say, You know about the computers.

I nod like a bobble-head doll. "We all mainlined the silicon chip like heroin addicts."

He looks at me strangely. Keep him guessing. For some reason I have the advantage. Sigi breaks the silence with my coffee. She puts it down a little too hard, spins on her heel and makes for the door.

"Anyway, that's over," he says after Sigi has gone in a huff.

"Yep." I take it as my cue to stand up. And pick up the box of Buddhas. He wants something more out of me and I'm not eager to go along. Another second and I'm liable to blow it.

"You're expected back right away?"

"Er . . . no." Expected by who? Suddenly I flash that the guy's scared. Why's he letting me take the Buddhas? Maybe he's not the boss after all.

"Then Sigi, I believe, has some documents to go back to the customs house." That thin smile again, it's driving me crazy. People must smile like that when they're sipping Danish liqueurs.

I stop at the door and put a touch of threat into my voice. "We won't let it happen again." Meaning *you*, pal.

The smile disappears. Exactly what I wanted. "Of course not," he says.

Now I'm sure about it. He's the little cheese. I narrow my eyes like a Hollywood Nazi and close the door. Right on cue the people in the big room stop working. Sigi looks worried. "It's okay," I say. "This time."

I'm pushing it, I always do. I say to Sigi, "Ingmar says you've got—"

She's already holding out a pair of manila envelopes with the company's name printed on the mailing labels. They want a messenger, I'll be a messenger. She follows me to the door.

"The computers will still be down tomorrow. Can you come back?"

I shrug. "Sure."

"It is like living in the Dark Ages here."

I agree with her. She sighs and holds open the door. I say, "Can I ask you a question?"

She nods, a little suspicious.

"What sport's he play?"

She glances over her shoulder, speaks almost in a whisper. "Curling," she says, like it's something sinister.

I get this image of Ingmar under a bubble-shaped hair dryer. "Curling?"

"It's played on ice."

"Oh."

She's in no hurry to go inside. I wait her out. Can't let her see me getting into the Checker. Messenger boys don't drive around in cabs.

Just as she's closing the door a car comes clanking into the lot. It's a rusty old-style station wagon, a surfer's woody. On the side it says RAPID ROGER—CITYWIDE MESSENGER SERVICE and a phone number. The guy driving is younger than me, nineteen maybe, a skinhead in a tie-dyed T-shirt. Most of the messengers in town are punkers. This one ratchets the parking brake and jumps out of the car. He's wearing camouflage pants and combat boots.

I intercept him ten feet from the door, Sigi still watching. "False alarm. Computers are back up. Sorry about the wasted trip."

The kid looks at me dully. He consults his clipboard. "Ingrid . . . uh, Morgenstern?"

"Right place, wrong dimension. Give over." I take the clipboard out of his hand and sign illegibly. When I hand it back there's a five-dollar bill under the clip.

He stares at the money as I guide him back to his car. "Somebody called for a messenger," he says. The motor's still running and his walkie-talkie's squawking on the seat. Now Sigi's out the door and walking toward us. "Go on," I tell him. "Get the fuck out of here."

But Sigi's right behind me. "Hello?" she says. "Can I help you?"

"Somebody called for a messenger," he says stubbornly,

like one of those dolls with a pull cord who says the same stupid phrase over and over.

"Wrong somebody," I start to say but Sigi's talking again.

"It's all right," she says. "I forgot to call and cancel. You can see we've already got one."

The kid reluctantly gets in the car. He's not programmed for this. Sigi goes back inside. I open his door on the passenger side and reach for the clipboard on the seat.

And take back my five bucks.

Eleven

IT ISN'T EASY FINDING the customs house. I don't even know *what* it is at first. Turns out to be U.S. Customs headquarters, Agent Bailey's command center, a three-story stone building at the bottom of the big hill near the northern waterfront. I half expect alarms to go off and a metal gate to come crashing down as I step inside, but nothing like that happens. A security guard points me down the hall to a room where I hand over the manila envelopes from Morgenstern to a sweet old lady with a big smile and a United Way pin, and get a receipt. No questions asked. On the way out I pass a fellow messenger, another punk rocker with a pompadour Mohawk, ripped T-shirt and studs on his boots. Ninety percent of life is looking the part.

Next I stop at a phone booth that still has a directory and look up Rollaway. My employer, according to Agent Bailey. I find nothing in the residential half, but the business section lists Cecil Rollaway, D.D.S., Rollaway Hide-a-Beds, and Rollaway Trucking. On the assumption that this isn't about a killer dentist or mattress salesman, I go with the trucker.

Rollaway Trucking is half a mile from Pier Street, close to the waterfront and a stone's throw from the abandoned grain elevator. There's a blacktopped yard with five or six big rigs parked parallel and a couple of diesel fuel pumps under a corrugated plastic awning. A big bearded man in coveralls and matching gimme cap is hosing down one of the trucks. The chromework is dull and pitted. In the northwest corner of the lot is a small prefab office with polarized shades to block direct sunlight.

I figure I'm not welcome inside so I sit in the Checker for an hour and watch events unfold, such as they are. The bearded man finishes spraying one of the trucks and starts on another. A cat pads across the yard. Clouds pass overhead in the shape of Mr. Clean and the Pillsbury Doughboy. And that's about it. Can't take the pace at Rollaway Trucking.

I haven't had enough of sitting in a stuffy automobile doing nothing so I drive up to the Heights and stake out my own place for two hours. Except for Huffington's chauffeur-driven limo, nobody comes or goes. Which is weird. It's been twenty-four hours since I left my wallet in Agent Bailey's hideout, and still no cops. I wonder what fiendish game they're playing. Finally I say screw it and coast down the driveway. Let the cops play their hand.

The garage door swings opens on cue. The Checker taps the 76 ball. I cut the engine and listen.

Getting out of the car I nearly break my neck falling over a stack of boxes. There are six of them, twelve-inch cubes all nice and white and uniform. They're sealed with strapping tape and one has a handwritten Post-it note stuck to it. I can't read the writing. Milo.

I slice open one of the boxes and pull out a handful of papers. They look like copies of a test, handwritten answers to mimeographed questions.

8. Write paragraph in which heroine is
   kissed by hero for first time.

*I tripped over the hoop of my ball dress and
fell back breathlessly against the divan, imprisoned in my cage of crinoline and lace.
My heart was pumping furiously! Surely he
could hear it! He came slowly toward me,
his doublet undone, his hair tousled wildly,
his razor-sharp sword dangling menacingly
in its gilded sheath . . .*

I climb over the boxes to the phone and dial. It rings the
customary twenty times.

"Yes?"

"Milo—Jack."

"Oh, hello, Jack."

" '*Hello,* Jack'? Is that all you can say? With me living in
a U-Stor-It garage?"

"Is merely me being polite."

"What have I got here, Milo? No, I know exactly what
I've got."

"Jack, no! Do not open the boxes!"

"What is it, radioactive waste?"

"No, no."

"You're moonlighting again." Milo won't admit it, won't
even tell his wife, but he loses money on the antiques business. His real job, the one that pays the bills, changes every
month.

"Do not disturb the boxes, Jack! Is exceedingly fragile."

"I already did. You're teaching romance-writing by correspondence course. Milo, you scamp."

"Is favor for a friend."

"Is inventory, Milo. You know I hate inventory."

"Oh, yes."

"You big baby. Just tell me how long I've got to live in Lego Land."

"Is not long now. Jack, I must go. There is a knock at the door."

Milo's way of getting off the phone. I tried it with Gina once and she threatened to beat the shit out of me. When I hang up, Putz is standing by the side door, eating a banana.

"Bitchen, man. What is it, art?"

"No, boxes. What's shaking, Putzboy?"

He shrugs, climbs into the Checker and presses the button on my hydraulic lift. The cab rises to the ceiling. He cranks open the window. "Nothin' much. Old man's on the war-path again."

"Listen, thanks for playing lookout for me last couple of days."

"It was nothin'. What do they want you for, anyway?"

"Death and dismemberment."

He laughs. What he doesn't realize, I don't always kid around. "Anyway there was somethin'," he says. "The same car went by a few times round about seven A.M. then stopped for a while down at the corner. That's all."

So they're on my trail after all. It's almost a relief. "Car? What kind of car?"

"Dark green VW Rabbit with a dent in the rear right fender. Here's the license plate."

A piece of paper floats down. "Hey, Jack. Went to the comic book store today? Guess what they got."

"Uh, comics?"

"Issue number one of *Blaster Boy,* man. Stone perfect condition in protective plastic. Guess the price."

"You got me. Fifty bucks?"

"A hundred and seventy-five, man."

"No kidding? Shit, I'd beg borrow or steal to get my hands on that one." Only five hundred copies printed before they yanked it off the newsstands. My collection only goes back to issue fifteen.

"Yeah," he says dreamily. Kid has his priorities straight. "Also Gina came by," he says, trying to sound casual. "She was acting pretty pissed off." Putz has a crush on Gina.

"You gonna call her, Jack?"

"Don't you have any homework to do?"

"This for the customs house. This for the FDA. And this for XYZ Electronics. Somebody apparently doesn't know how to fill out a simple form. Goddamn *fucking* computer!"

Talk like that doesn't sound right coming out of Sigi's mouth. I see her yodeling sweetly in the Black Forest somewhere. She's like Heidi after her hormones kicked in.

Today she's wearing a tight, kelly green velveteen skirt with a loopy gold chain hanging low on her hips. Gina would like that part. Just the top button of her blouse is open. She's demure. Her necklace is this finely carved chain with figures which look like dancing dwarfs. Her earrings are fat gold hoops.

Everybody's a little nervous around me today, as if I'm about to spray the room with machine-gun fire. Ingmar's been shut up in his office all morning. I've come and gone three times. They want me on hand so I sit in the lunchroom and read the paper between errands. Only Richard acts like he's not afraid of me. He's the one with the bush baby on his head. The computer repairman is nowhere to be seen.

At lunchtime I pass by the older guy with the half-glasses and the cardigan sweater. He's got a pocket chess set out on the desk. Next to it is a liverwurst sandwich in neatly creased wax paper.

"Looks like Kretschmar's defense in Barcelona in '57," I say. "Wiped the room with Ivanov."

He looks up in surprise. His name is Ted. He peers over his glasses. "You play?"

"Strictly amateur. I'd be no match for you."

Ted says something like "Humph" and goes back to his board. But he's softening up.

Eight hours of this and some clever banter with Sigi and I'm no closer to finding out who's the real boss. I can't ask straight out because I'm supposed to know. Ingmar comes out of his office every once in a while but hardly seems to notice me. It's like I've worked there for years. I'm family.

At 3 P.M. comes the call from the computer guy. Betty takes it, her bracelets clattering all over the desk when she lunges for the phone. She says the company's name and follows up with a couple of uh-huhs. Then her face lights up. "Hey, everybody," she calls out. "Repairman'll be here first thing tomorrow morning!"

Everybody cheers except me.

Round about four-thirty I palm a key from reception along with the phone number and code of their alarm service. Not long after that I get permission to go. Everybody else is right behind me, Sigi last locking up. Ingmar drives a BMW, Richard a Cherokee 4×4, Sigi a Mazda 626, Ted a Kawasaki 350. Betty the receptionist is picked up by her husband, a cargo handler for United Airlines, in a Firebird.

I drive over to a hotel coffee shop near the airport. They have a special on strawberries. They've got strawberry pancakes, strawberry waffles, strawberry shortcake, strawberry pâté. There's a forest of full-color cardboard strawberries hanging from the ceiling on strings. I figure they must have got stuck with a consignment of nearly rotten strawberries. Happened to me once.

I eschew the strawberries and order a cup of coffee and a bran muffin. Ride around all day on the hard seat of a Checker, you've got to stay regular. I kill another hour at the airport watching the planes come and go. I could do that all day. Then I head back to Ingmar Morgenstern & Co., Inc. It's still light out and there may be pool supply people next door, which is all the better for me. Nobody looks twice at suspicious characters in the daytime.

The alarm goes off as I open the door. I flick a switch under the reception desk and call the alarm company. The girl is exceedingly polite. I relock the door and start looking around.

Right away I hit a wall. Ingmar's office door is locked and I don't have the key. Judging from the way he treats Sigi, neither does she. I find a couple of hairpins and a paper clip in Betty's drawer that do the trick.

All the file cabinets are locked. This guy is lock-happy. The hairpins don't work on the cabinets. But they do open the top drawer in Ingmar's desk, and there's a set of keys inside.

The file cabinets are crammed full of invoices, receipts, letters from banks and bureaucrats, bills of lading. Ingmar has absolutely no room to expand. I find Al Merkel's file in the third drawer and run down the list of things he's imported over the years. It's all cheap novelty items from Taiwan, Korea, China, and India with names like X-Ray Robo Man and Sobbing Sally Ann. Psycho Mickey fits right in. But there's nothing about any screaming Buddhas.

In the desk are a bunch of receipts from messenger services and a set of books, but that's about it. That plus hundreds of names in a double-wheeled Rolodex. I sit back and stare at Ingmar's curling trophies. Who is this guy? A customs broker who's been scamming Customs somehow. Dope, microchips, phony Barbie dolls . . . could be anything. I ought to check his Rolodex.

Voices in the main room. I didn't hear anybody come in because a plane was going overhead. Like everybody else I've stopped noticing the planes. It's a woman's voice coming closer to the door of Ingmar's office, saying "Sigi never forgets—"

Betty opens the door and screams.

Twelve

ACTUALLY IT'S MORE OF A SQUEAK. Like a hamster that's been thrown against the wall.

"Jack . . . ?"

"Betty. What are you doing here?"

I sound stern and suspicious. She gives a little start. "Me? I was just . . . I left a present for my husband . . ."

"Betty?" Her husband sticks his head in the door. It's the size and shape of a watermelon. He's six-three maybe, 220 pounds with a crew cut and wearing a football shirt with the number 89. He has an unusually high-pitched voice. "What's going on?"

Betty says, "It's Jack, Howie. Jack . . . Jack what?"

I stretch my neck like I'm trying to see past them. Fat chance, with Howie blocking the light. I say in a conspiratorial whisper, "Anybody else out there?"

Betty says, "No, but the alarm, how'd you get—"

"Good. I'm working on a little after-hours project. Ingmar's cooking up a surprise for Sigi."

"Ingmar? For Sigi?" She's processing.

"Sssh! No telling. Little birthday thing."

"But Sigi's birthday was last month. We had a big party. Jack, the alarm—"

"Ingmar let me in. He's ordering her some custom-made Danish furniture. Takes forever for it to come."

Howie steps farther into the room. "Is this the guy?" In that high and squeaky voice.

Betty groans. "Oh, shit, Howie, not *this* again!"

"It's him, right?" He shrugs his shoulders and takes another step toward me.

"Oh, Howie, get real. Bill Duray's the guy, I mean he's the guy who *wasn't* the guy. I never did anything with Bill Duray!"

Howie's eyes narrow. His voice gets even higher when he's pissed off. "Not Bill Duray? *This* motherfucker? Motherfucking *Jack?*" My name comes out in a way I don't like.

"For Christ's sake, Howie, I don't even know his last name!"

For some reason this makes things worse. Howie's hands are opening and closing like man-eating plants. I wheel slowly backward toward the trophy case.

"I'm warning you, Howie." Betty's voice is deeper than her husband's, full of authority. "Back off."

Howie thinks about it for a few days. Slowly he backs away, body stiff, eyes on mine, jaw slack. Tough guy. Meet you after school at the bike racks. Betty lets him by.

"I'll just go get that present," she says to nobody.

I ask her to wait. "Listen, Betty, do me a favor, won't you? Don't tell Ingmar I told you about the furniture. He'll kill me for it."

Betty nods. The toughness is gone and she seems a bit unsure of herself. Howie brings out the best in her. "You . . . you're . . ."

"Go on."

"What *is* your last name, anyway?"

"Squire. Jack Squire."

Another nod. Then she goes.

From the look on Howie's face I figure I'd better go, too. And leave Ingmar's Rolodex behind.

Driving home I have a vision of Betty naked.

I stop off at the building on Pier Street where Agent Bailey was killed. It's been two days since the murder and the place is still sealed with police tape. The wall of windows is dark. I don't see any cops.

I go around to the alley behind the building to confirm the existence of a back door. How the killer came and went. Then I cross the street to the warehouse where I found the green container. It's a long, low structure with a door big enough to drive a truck through, which I guess is the point. There's also a smaller door for people, painted orange with a security company sticker.

The sky has gone dark and the street's deserted, so I don't trouble myself over the time it takes to crack the lock with the help of Betty's hairpins. After a few minutes it snaps open. Would have thought they'd have a better lock.

I pull the door shut behind me and wait for my eyes to adjust but it's totally black inside. No alarm goes off. I switch on my penlight, illuminating a circle of bare and dusty wooden floor. I raise the light and it falls on a beat-up truck chassis, a twenty-foot steel frame on wheels.

Other than that, the warehouse is empty.

I'm not the only one who hates inventory.

I get to work next morning by eight-thirty and the computer repairman is already there. The guts of a CPU are spilling out all over the floor. Richard hovers over the repairman with a jelly doughnut like one guy advising another guy on the barbeque. I grab the last doughnut in the coffee room and settle into a corner with the sports page. I figure I keep quiet, they'll forget I'm there.

Betty comes in for a cup of coffee and gives me kind of a funny look. I answer with a wink. Her hair looks rushed this morning, but then it always does. She says, "I'm supposed to get your Social Security number."

"I'll bring it in tomorrow." Got to figure out which one I haven't used for a while.

Later on Sigi comes in and I decide it's time to quit with the invisibility act.

"Guten Tag," I say.

She looks surprised. "You speak German?"

"Not really. Picked up a smattering of languages with Special Forces. Enough to get by. Want part of my jelly doughnut?"

"Ugh." She's searching around for the Sweet'n Low. Today she's wearing a sea green cashmere mock turtleneck with a snug navy blue woolen skirt and one-inch heels. She's a strapping young girl.

"Ingmar, does he speak German?"

She finds the sweetener and proceeds to empty ten of the little packets into her coffee. "Aaah, noooo."

"Danish, then. He seems Danish."

"He speaks English to me." She sweeps the torn pink papers into the wastebasket.

"You must have worked with him a long time. I mean, the way he trusts you with running the office and all."

She lets out a tight little snort. "Ingmar keeps his business to himself."

"You mean you guys never just sit around and shoot the breeze over a glass of peppermint schnapps?"

Sigi shivers.

"Small office like this one, I'm surprised. People get to know each other. Birthday parties, company picnics, baby showers. Everybody doing a little of everything. Whereas in a big company, it's like that factory in *Metropolis,* you know that German flick where everybody marches back and forth like robots? Twenty years of punching a clock and you never see the boss."

"I could do more." Sigi pulls out a chair and sits at the table, nodding at her coffee as she stirs, almost talking to herself. "I could do a lot more, if he'd let me."

"Well, there you are. Some people don't know how to delegate. This thing with the Buddhas, for instance. How'd that happen, anyway?"

She shrugs. "A few days ago Ingmar comes storming out of his office, saying we lost a container, we lost a container, how could we lose another goddamn container? I say, Ingmar, how should I know? This is your personal account. Nobody knows anything about it except you."

"You never would have let that happen."

"That's right." Her voice is firm and very German. *Jawohl, mein Herr.*

"What I'm saying. Bring in the right people and let 'em rip. It's this whole quality thing."

She leans toward me. "Once I say to him, I say, Ingmar, one day you are going to have a really big disaster. He won't even learn to use the computer, it's all in his head, *ja?* I say Ingmar, maybe we should X-ray that head of yours. What if should you be in a terrible accident? What should we do then? But he won't listen. I say all I can say."

And suddenly here's Ingmar himself, standing in the doorway like the guest of honor at a wake.

Sigi straightens up, tosses her hair back. No telling what he's heard.

"Mr. Squire," he says softly. "Would you come in my office, please."

I follow him out to the main room. The computer repairman flicks a switch and all the screens light up together.

Everybody claps except the repairman, me, Ingmar, and Sigi in the doorway leading to the coffee room.

Inside his office Ingmar picks up an envelope from the desk. "Thank you for your help. Here is one last job for you. If you could please take this back to him."

He hands me the envelope. It's blank on the outside, except for the Morgenstern logo embossed in the corner.

I wait. Ingmar waits. He looks depressed.

"Okay?" he says.

"Okay."

Sigi pokes her head in the doorway. Could have been out there listening. She says to Ingmar, "Your mother called earlier. When you were on the phone."

Immediately he goes to his phone and punches two buttons. Good sons keep their moms on speed dial. As I'm going out he says, "Hello, Mama."

Three days of loyal service, and he doesn't even shake my hand. Those cold Danes.

Thirteen

TAKE IT TO HIM. Whoever the hell "him" is.

First thing I do is go home and open the envelope. I would have grabbed a spare blank but Ingmar watched me go. As it is I have to steam it open and hope nobody will notice. You'd be surprised how unobservant people can be.

I'm leaning over my little hot plate when the phone rings. I almost drop the envelope into the pot.

"Hello, Jack."

"Gina! Been meaning to call."

"What'd you do, slip into another dimension?"

"It's been known to happen."

"Or maybe you're still here and I just didn't notice. Damn, I forgot to check under the refrigerator."

"It turned out not to be safe."

"I'll grant you that, Jack. I can be very dangerous."

"How about a replay tonight? I'll bring over a bottle of grappa. We'll get snockered."

Silence. Gina deciding whether she's still angry. "Saturday. I need a model."

"Indoors, right? And fully clothed."

"No and no."

"Ouch. Don't you ever forget what a prize I am, Gina."

"Yeah, like one of those whirly rings in a box of Cracker Jack."

I've been forgiven. "I happen to like Cracker Jack. Broke my heart when they stopped selling it at the ballpark."

"Eight A.M., Jack. It's a long drive."

And she hangs up. Gina can be a hard woman. Fortunately I'm an easy kind of guy.

"Gina coming over?"

That's Putz. He's lying on the futon eating Screaming Yellow Zonkers and watching *The Frugal Gladiator*. He's brought down his algebra homework just for show.

"No Gina tonight, Putz. Sorry to let you down."

He gives a heavy sigh. He doesn't realize that Gina would eat him alive. By now the envelope has turned crackly from the steam and opens easily. Inside is a single sheet of Morgenstern letterhead. It's a list of ship names, followed by dates going back to the beginning of the year, and extending into the next three months. With departures every other month or so, no arrivals, which doesn't make sense. If he's an importer, why would he care when the ship leaves?

There's no name or address inside. I'm supposed to know where it goes. Take it to *him*.

Back to Morgenstern's, blow off the risk. I tell Putz to help himself to a frozen burrito and take off. If I don't deliver the letter they'll know, they may already. At most I've got till morning. So I do the thing with the alarm company again and take my chances.

It's eleven at night and the pool supply people are gone. I search for a hidden safe or strongbox with the private file of this mystery man or woman. I look behind pictures, under the throw rug, in the file cabinets again. Nothing suggests itself. I start rifling through the Rolodex. It's hopeless, any one of these hundreds of names could be the right one. No way to check it out this late at night.

Sigi said Ingmar keeps it all in his head, no written records unless he absolutely has to. He must have some other way of communicating, other than by messenger. He must talk to this person all the time.

Speed dial. I pick up Ingmar's phone, press # and 1. It's ringing! Too bad it's after midnight. On the fifth ring, somebody picks up.

"Hello." A man with a sleepy voice.

Shit, it's Ingmar. I've reached his home. I give him a few lines of phony Chinese and hang up.

#2 rings with no answer. #3 gets a pissed-off Sigi. #4 gets a husky female voice.

"Hi," she says.

"Hi." Sounds like I woke her, too, but she's happy about it.

"Been thinking about you," she says.

"And me of you."

"Comfortable?"

I sit back in Ingmar's creaky chair. "Sure."

"Mmmm. Me too. Let's get the boring part out of the way. Which credit card you using tonight?"

"Another time, okay?" That Ingmar.

#5 gets the answering machine of the messenger service. #6 gets a nice old lady with a Danish accent. Ingmar's mom. I apologize for waking her up. I wonder if she knows her son ranks her sixth.

#7 and #8 aren't programmed. I'm about to hang up on #9 when somebody answers on the tenth ring.

"Yeah."

Deep voice, a little touch of Brooklyn in the night. Sounds rushed but he wasn't asleep.

"Sir?"

"Fuck you." And hangs up in my ear.

This is a serious breach of telephone etiquette, I don't care what time it is. I call back.

He says, "Who the fuck is this?" One thing for certain, he ain't Danish.

"Federal Express, sir. We have a package with your number on it but the address is obscured. Would you kindly confirm it for us?"

"At fucking half past midnight?"

"We never sleep, sir."

"Who's it from?"

"That, too, sir, is unreadable. The package has been through a storm."

More swearing. But he gives me the address. Some place down on the piers.

"Yes, that looks right."

"And wait till fucking morning to deliver it."

I'm seriously tempted to say something nasty, but I restrain myself.

"Thank you, sir. You have been most kind."

He hangs up, most unkindly.

The office is inside one of the last covered piers still standing south of the bridge. The rest either burned down or the buildings were demolished because they were about to collapse anyway. The sun's just peeking over the hills across the bay and spilling orange light onto the pier. The air is cool and sweet with the smell of kelp and marine fuel.

It was those two unprogrammed numbers on Ingmar's speed dial that did it for me. A three-number gap between his mother and Joe Rude, the mystery guy he puts on the end. Lucky number nine. I sit in the cab with a bucket of 7-Eleven coffee and a box of powdered doughnuts and watch people go into the building. At nine-fifteen I follow them in.

From the top of the stairs a carpeted mezzanine stretches the length of the pier. Down the right side is a row of offices, down the left a railing overlooking the open floor, which has been converted into an indoor parking lot. The ceiling's high and curved and full of crisscrossing beams like a European train station. The mezzanine's done up in pastel blues and whites, very nautical.

It's cold inside. I pass a couple of travel agencies, a design firm, the Prune Advisory Board, they give advice on prunes. Then another customs broker, an import-export firm, and at the very end, Suite 225, Thacker Enterprises.

The door has a pebbled glass window and a sign that says ENTER for people who can't figure it out. Just to make things interesting, the door is locked. I can see a shape moving around inside. I knock on the glass.

The shape keeps moving but nobody answers. I knock harder. The shape stops at the door. I tap once more and the shape opens up.

The shape is a woman. She's about twenty-one, five feet tall with a ballet dancer's body and electric blond hair. She has very pale skin, wide cheekbones and enormous eyes. I picture her floating onto the open palm of some big-muscled Baryshnikov. With all that hair she's like a beautiful dust bunny.

She stands in the doorway. I hold up a fresh envelope with Morgenstern's logo in the corner. In the dead of night I remembered to grab a spare. "For the boss," I say.

"Oh." She stares at the envelope like it's a jar of honey and I'm a steel-clawed beartrap.

"Personal delivery."

No names. I can't take a chance on there really being a Thacker.

She throws up her hands and opens the door wide. A message for the boss! This whole thing is too much for her.

She leaves me standing in the middle of the room and goes

through a door to the left. "From Morgenstern," I hear her say. I walk over to the windows which look out on the bay. The light's so strong I can barely see. There are eight desks in the room and all but one are spotless, each with its phone and blotter and Post-it note dispenser, leather pencil cup and Webster's pocket hyphenation guide.

The one messy desk is in a corner opposite the windows, near the door the girl just went through. Wedged into the corner beside the desk is the biggest rubber plant I've ever seen outside the rain forest. One of the fronds leans over her chair like a subway commuter sneaking a look at your evening paper. On the credenza there's an electric type-writer humming away with a piece of paper in it. The paper says THACKER ENTERPRISES but that's all I can read.

I perch my butt on one of the clean desks near the windows but stand up the minute she comes back because I don't like the way she looks about it. Right behind her is a muscular middle-aged man, about five-six with a leathery tan and close-cropped white hair. He's wearing a tight ma-roon Crocodile shirt and creased khakis with woven belt and Top-Siders. He doesn't walk, he pads, with a center of gravity three inches above his belly button. The Preppy Thug.

"Hunh," he says, so I know we can at least communicate in sounds. Then, "Patricia."

Patricia looks like she's about to go *en pointe* and screw herself into the floor. But she goes back to her desk and resumes typing.

The man taps twice on the desk I'm standing next to. I catch a whiff of Old Spice. "Take this one," he says. Okay with me, it's got a view. There's even room for Agent Bailey's family pictures.

"All right?" he says, palms out, like it's another major crisis solved. His fifth and sixth words since we met. This isn't the guy on the phone. His accent falls somewhere between London and Newport News.

Already he's headed back into his office. I say, "Don't I need to fill out a W-4?"

He stops for a second and glowers at me. Then he goes into the office and shuts the door.

I look over at Patricia. "Thacker, right?"

She's typing away, her shoulders hunched up, trying to keep from brushing against the rubber plant. She's afraid of it.

"Right," she says.

Fourteen

YOU WALK INTO A PLACE, nobody knows you from Adam, they hire you. So that's how you get a job.

I spend the morning staring out the window and reading the pocket hyphenation guide. Patricia barely speaks to me. She types and types and the letterhead forms pile up in her OUT basket. The clock tower chimes on the hour. A ferryboat horn blasts every forty minutes.

Thacker, whose first name is Frank, stays in his office. Twice the phone rings, Patricia answers it, and buzzes the call through. She has this big clip in her hair, a rainbow with dancing music notes. I'm getting to know it.

I say, "Lot of people out sick today."

Patricia barely slows down. "No," she says. "Nobody's sick."

"Vacation, then."

A single shake of the head, left-right.

"Man." I put down the hyphenation book at con-cu-pis-cence. "You mean you hold down this madhouse all by yourself?"

She nods, seven quick ones.

"I was thinking I'd run out and get a cup of coffee. You want anything?"

Her fingers hang over the keys like a pianist ready to strike the opening chord. "I think it's better you stick around."

"Lunch is when?"

"Noon." She's getting irritated. What does she expect, with no employee manual?

"You really know your way around this place," I say. "Been here long?"

"Oh!" She's made a mistake. She yanks open a drawer and digs around for some whiteout. In the process her hair brushes against the rubber plant. Her body twitches as if she'd stuck her finger in a light socket.

"Might be a good idea to move that thing," I say.

Her hands are shaking as she applies a drop of whiteout to the paper. She doesn't fear the rubber plant. She dreads it.

I don't want to lose the conversational momentum. "How was it, working with Michael?"

Her head jerks toward me. She moves like a hummingbird. "Michael?"

"Yeah, you know, the last messenger. Whatever happened to him, anyway?"

Thacker's office door opens and out comes Thacker. He's carrying a package the size of a Kleenex box, wrapped in brown paper and string.

He puts it on my desk. "Take this to the airport. International terminal. Follow the signs to the lockers." He places a numbered key on the top of the package.

"Then what?"

"Then you come back."

"Mind if I stop for lunch on the way back?"

"Of course."

Of course I mind, Of course you can stop—I can't tell which he means. But he doesn't seem to like questions.

So I don't ask any more.

The package is strangely light. I place it against my ear to see if it's ticking.

I have a secret shortcut from this part of town to the freeway involving a couple of parking lots and a one-way street. So it doesn't take long for me to realize I'm being followed. The driver is a lousy tail. The car is a dark green VW Rabbit.

Instead of taking the freeway I head up a big hill south of downtown that's heavily residential with plenty of alleys and steep streets. I stop at a random apartment house with a recessed entrance and press all the buttons. Right away the buzzer sounds and I go inside. I climb a flight of stairs, wait half a minute, and go back out. The Rabbit is down at the corner with one wheel on the curb. Subtle.

I get back in the Checker. Either I get rid of the package or get rid of the Rabbit. I do a couple of fancy loops and switchbacks. When last seen the Rabbit is headed the other way.

I pull into an alley and examine the package. It's your basic brown paper package with string, unmarked and nicely wrapped. The knot's too tight to undo, I'll have to cut it. Which means buying some more string. This is getting complicated.

I find the string at a corner market and carefully unwrap the package. As a kid at Christmas I was the champ at peeking into presents. The hard part is faking surprise.

No need to fake it now. It's the shoebox from a two-hundred-dollar pair of cross-trainers. The box is stuffed with tissue paper. I smooth out the paper on my thigh, hold it up to the light. No cryptic hieroglyphs. I put the tissue paper back in the box and rewrap it carefully. Then I drive out to the airport and make Thacker's delivery.

On my way back I grab a copy of the afternoon paper. There's a profile of Ray Bailey on page one. CUSTOMS MYSTERY MAN, it says. Evidently he once applied for the job of Special Agent. Before that he tried to become a cop, then a security guard. All three times he was eighty-sixed, thanks to a ten-year-old conviction for possession and sale of marijuana. The sort of thing that dogs you for life.

Eventually Bailey had to settle for input clerk down at the pier, tapping away at a keyboard all day long. Friends said he was a nice man, couldn't imagine him getting mixed up in a drug deal. He loved cop shows, used to listen to the police band on his shortwave. No comment from Mrs. Bailey, who has left town to be with friends.

Ray Bailey would have made a great cop. If you ask me, he already was.

I sacrifice a sandwich for the time it takes to call a friend at the DMV and run down the license plate from the green Rabbit. Anytime a private detective says he's got a friend at the DMV, it's this guy. Actually he doesn't work there anymore, he was forcibly retired after twenty years of running the computer room. Now he keeps a private connection from his home. His name is Lou, and that's all you need to know.

Lou has Muzak on hold. I didn't know you could get it at home. Right now it's playing "Smoke on the Water."

"Jack?"

"Still here."

"The plates belong to a Ruby Wong, two-five-eight Forty-seventh Avenue. That's out near the beach. She wears corrective lenses."

The nefarious nearsighted Ruby Wong. "Thanks, Lou."

"My pleasure." Another chance to stick it to his former employer.

Back in the office I spend the afternoon catching up on my back issues of *Cab and Cabbie*. There's a big debate over radio versus computer dispatchers, a tribute to the beaded seat cushion, a comparison of the top ten liquid air fresheners. There should be a copy right there on the seat, you can take it home. Meanwhile Patricia cowers beneath the rubber plant.

Headed home at five o'clock I plan my busy evening. First some Hunan bean curd from the Happy Assassin, then a drive out to the home of Ruby Wong and a midnight visit to Thacker Enterprises. I have a strong feeling that I'm closing in.

I top the rise of the driveway and fly down the slope. I come this close to rear-ending the police car parked in front of the garage.

The cop inside is writing on a clipboard so he doesn't notice that he almost got turned into a human accordion. Patrol cars are getting flimsier and the Checker is the nearest a civilian can come to armored transport. Now the cop sees me in his rearview mirror. He climbs lazily out of the car and hikes up his gunbelt. He has a small gray moustache and sunburned cheeks. He's nearly fifty, still trim and nicely groomed.

About time you showed up, I think, while my brain races to concoct a story. Stay loose, Jack.

"Evening, Officer."

"And you are?"

"That's right."

The cop looks disgusted. "Your *name*."

As if he didn't know it. "Squire. Jack Squire."

He nods, makes a note on the clipboard. "You live here, Mr. Squire?"

"In the garage, yeah."

The garage door is wide open. I got rid of the bloody clothes, but the pictures of Agent Bailey's family are in plain sight. News flash: Squire kicked out of Mensa. I feel in my pocket for a quarter to call my lawyer.

"That your cab, sir?"

I don't like the *sir*. "Yes, Officer, it's mine. Fully insured and paid for."

He frowns. I've violated rule number one: Don't answer what you weren't asked. Settle down.

"Mr. Squire, have you seen anyone in the neighborhood lately who doesn't belong here?"

Other than me? "You mean like suspicious characters?"

"Anyone loitering, cruising, walking back and forth, checking out the houses."

Other than a cop in a green VW Rabbit? "What happened, Officer?"

"Mr. Ronald Huffington has reported a theft."

"No shit? What'd they get, money, jewels, what? You're saying somebody broke in?" In books people are always sputtering and that's what I'm doing now. The only time I act suspicious is when I'm innocent.

The cop looks at me funny. "I didn't say anything about a break-in, sir."

"I just meant—"

"Although we can assume there was one."

"Exactly what I was saying."

"Mr. Huffington lost a rare silver tray. A gift from the king of Sweden."

He gave him things that he was needin'. "He's sure it was stolen?"

"It was there last night. And gone this morning."

"No, Officer, I didn't see anything suspicious."

The cop writes on his clipboard for a long time. I know what he's thinking: ex-con living in the house of a million-

93

aire, millionaire loses priceless silver tray, you figure it out. I feel for Agent Bailey.

The cop finishes writing with a flourish, clicks his pen and fastens the sheet to the clipboard. He's trying to act casual about looking into the open garage. He takes a step inside, makes it look accidental.

"Officer? Mind if I put my car in?"

"If I could just have your phone number, sir."

I give it to him and he writes it down. Finally he opens the door of his car. Then he stops and stares at me.

"Haven't I seen you somewhere before?"

I shrug. "I couldn't say, Officer."

I've barely got the words out when I recognize him. It's the cop who was directing traffic outside the warehouse when I drove over to get my wallet back. The Checker has tickled his memory. Two more seconds and he'll have it nailed.

"Well," I say, "so long," and climb into the Checker and back up the slope. The cop shakes his head, then gets into his own car. At the top of the driveway he steals one last glance at me before heading off down the street.

I take a deep breath, feel that spurt of adrenaline.

Which clears one thing up at least. The police don't have my wallet.

Whoever killed Agent Bailey does.

Fifteen

■■
■■

I PUT OFF DINNER AND DRIVE out toward the ocean around dusk to check on the green Rabbit's license plate. You'd think this neighborhood would be the most expensive part of Our Fair City, but you'd be wrong. It's mostly two-bedroom houses in pseudo-Spanish styling with microscopic lawns and wrought iron gates. Either that or blocky two-flat buildings with illegal mothers-in-law down. They call them Irish Contractors' Specials even though they're mostly built by the Chinese these days.

Ruby Wong's street runs west-east so the wind comes howling up from the beach. Big wads of fog swirl overhead like a storm scene in time-lapse photography. In the Heights it's clear and balmy. Which helps to explain the difference in property values.

Ruby is kind enough to park her car in the driveway. Either that or she can't fit the thing in her garage. Anyway the license plate matches up with the car that's been following me. Only one problem, it's a different car. Ruby drives an Olds Delta 88 which is so big it overlaps the strips of grass on either side and the sidewalk behind. It's about as inconspicuous as a bright yellow Checker Marathon.

I check the front of her car and see that the license plate's missing. The Rabbit may be a lousy tail but he's no fool. Probably has a whole collection.

I drive down to the beach and sit on the seawall and watch a Chinese father and son fly a dragon kite which must be fifty feet long. The kid's no more than four and wears a grown-up's down jacket which swallows him up. The kite swoops and dives like a drunken jet fighter.

Later I get my plate of Hunan bean curd, extra spicy. My fortune reads: WHEN THE BUDDHA IS SILENT IT IS MOST PRO- FOUND. Damn straight. After dinner I cross the street to catch a kung-fu movie from Hong Kong without subtitles, they're better that way. Finally it's late enough to try back at Thacker Enterprises. I call ahead just to make sure. The phone just goes on ringing.

All's quiet down at the pier, foghorns blasting away. The big parking lot underneath the covered pier is nearly empty. I'm way too conspicuous on the mezzanine but there's no one around. Every office is dark, Thacker's included.

He doesn't have an alarm system. Security here is for shit. The room is bathed in orange from the sodium vapor lights outside. The view tonight is spectacular, thousands of glow- ing dots on the hills across the bay.

I hear a humming, low and steady. Maybe there's an alarm after all, hot-wired to central dispatch, patrol cars rolling. I'm giving serious thought to cutting out when I notice that Patricia's electric typewriter is still on, humming away, as if she just stepped out for a cup of coffee. I wonder if she sleeps in her clothes.

Slowly I push open Thacker's unlocked office door. There's a big metal desk in the middle of the room. Sitting on the desktop in the orange light, along with a box of Pink Pearl erasers, is a screaming Buddha.

He's staring at me like a curio to scare off evil spirits.

Luckily I'm immune. There isn't much else in the room: an empty wire IN basket, a padded metal chair on rollers, plastic floor guard, the same Evergreen Lines calendar that was in Ingmar's office, a framed photograph of a sailboat, a couple of metal armchairs for visitors, and a safe.

It's a very unsubtle safe. No one has bothered to disguise it as a Franklin stove or a file cabinet, or hide it behind a crappy landscape. The thing is dark and square, two feet high, like a miniature of the black slab from *2001*. It practically shouts: Valuable Shit Inside! Like my wallet maybe.

But the safe has no dial, or keyhole, or any other obvious means of getting the door open. Just a pinprick of a hole on the door. I look behind, underneath and around, run my hands all over the pebbled surface. I'm no expert on safes but I've seen a few in my day, and not one looked like this.

It must work electronically, like a car alarm, and Thacker's got the controls. Short of rustling up some C-4, I'm out of luck.

I lean back in Thacker's chair and stare at the framed photo of the sailboat. In the dim light I can almost see the sails unfurling. I picture him sitting in a deck chair in the South Pacific, maybe the Caribbean, drinking funny-colored drinks. The whole scenario makes me mad. In frustration I grab the Buddha on his desk and give it a squeeze. Over in the corner, the safe opens.

That little hole in the door—not a keyhole. A sound-activated lock. The Buddha laughs at me.

There's no wallet in the safe, but there are a couple of thin files. I take them over to the desk and spread out the sheets of paper.

Some are on Morgenstern's letterhead. They look like a record of several dozen shipments to Hong Kong going back about five years—date, time, container number, and ship. With checkmarks next to every fifth or sixth shipment.

I reach into my pocket and unfold the sheet of paper that I intercepted from Ingmar to Thacker. The list of sailings matches up with the checked-off shipments in the files.

Back to the files. The contents are classified as TOYS. Toys, my eye. If I were a little kid, got one of those grinning Buddhas for Christmas, I'd be in a cold sweat for weeks.

Still, it's weird to be shipping toys to Hong Kong. Like selling rice to Japan. One hell of a market opportunity.

Even stranger, the container numbers next to the checkmarks keep on repeating. Thacker seems to be using the same three containers, over and over. Long odds on that. How many thousands of those things travel back and forth across the Pacific every day? What does he do, make a special request?

Now that I notice, everything else about those checked shipments is the same, too—same number of cartons, same exact weight. Maybe, I think, maybe they're the same Buddhas. The Zen way of exporting.

Last in the files are some papers which look like authorizations for retrieving shipments from the piers. The numbers square with the checked-off containers, which never seem to have gotten on any ship at all. Pulled back every time before they sailed. And thrown in with a bunch of legitimate shipments—other clients of Ingmar's—so nobody will notice.

Zen is the right word. Thacker's shipments are like his brown paper packages: empty. He's trucking the same three containers to and from the piers while the transaction—the sale and shipment of Buddhas—takes place only on paper. It's your basic money-laundering scam, with Frank Thacker as your friendly neighborhood Laundromat for dirty cash.

I made off with one of his three containers. So where are the other two?

On the way out, I turn off Patricia's typewriter.

*　*　*

Nine A.M. finds her already typing away. Probably picked up right in the middle of a sentence.

"Morning," I say and place a steaming cup of coffee on her desk, then packets of sugar and nondairy creamer and a stir stick on top of that.

"Uh . . . good morning." She looks startled, but she's easy to startle. Today she's wearing a bright red blouse with a big bow and an off-white skirt. I feel like sprinkling glitter in her hair.

"Sleep well?" I ask.

"Uh . . . yes." She flicks the lid off her coffee and empties the sugar and creamer into it.

I hang my jacket on the back of my chair and start rolling up my sleeves. "Well," I say. "Here goes nothing."

"Huh," she says, stirring her coffee.

"Always takes me a while to get down a routine. I imagine Michael had his own. Which desk was his, anyway?"

"Michael?"

Each day we start over. "Michael, yeah. My predecessor."

"Oh."

"Where'd he come from, anyway? I mean, how'd Thacker come to hire him?"

Still stirring the coffee. "One day he just walked in. He was a bicycle messenger."

"You remember what company he worked for?"

She shakes her head. "He was like, you know. One of those guys with funny hair and a rhinestone dog collar."

Your basic punk rocker/bike messenger. That could be useful. "And Thacker hired him on the spot?"

She nods.

"To do what?"

"Deliver packages. Just like you do."

"Then what happened?"

"What?"

99

"To Michael. Why'd he leave?"

She thinks about it. "He came back after lunch one day looking, I don't know, nervous. Nervous and upset. Around three o'clock he walked out and that was the end of it. He never came back after that."

"What did Thacker do?"

"He hired you." She looks at me like, Are you brain-dead or what?

I give a big yawn and stretch my arms. "I feel energetic today. You need any filing done? Invoices alphabetized? I worry that my talents are being underutilized."

She looks up from her coffee with big brown eyes, clouding over from the steam. "You'll . . . have to ask . . ."

"Thacker, yeah. Listen, Patricia, I just want to ask one more question. It's one of those trivial, niggling, insignificant little questions that rookies always ask their second day on the job. You mind?"

"No."

"What does Thacker Enterprises *do*?"

That startled look again. "I . . . well, you know, I . . . type up these invoices . . ."

She trails off like the job is so monumental she can't find the words to describe it.

Jack homes in, the human buzz saw. "Yeah, but invoices for *what*? Chewing gum? Pork bellies? Collapsible flanges, *what*?"

She gives it hard thought. "But . . . I thought you knew."

She's convinced this is some kind of a test. Casually I walk over and lift an invoice off the stack beside her typewriter. It's all numbers and letters and abbreviations, the typing's flawless. Patricia's hand flutters toward the paper. She says, "You'd better—" just as the door to Thacker's office opens and out comes Thacker. He looks grim.

His eyes travel from me to Patricia and back again. She

grabs the paper out of my hand and puts it back on the stack.

"I was just saying," I said. "Maybe you'd like somebody to dust that rubber plant."

Thacker stands there as if waiting for a translator to tell him what I just said. Then he hands me another wrapped package, a bit bigger than the last one but just as light.

"Here's the address," he says, holding out a piece of paper. "Just leave it by the door." The tone of his voice says he doesn't give a damn.

The address is neatly printed. The writer pressed so hard he broke through the paper. The place is on the big hill with the famous tower overlooking the Italian neighborhood. I hate driving up there, too many tourists looking for cabs.

I say, "You want this done first, or the rubber plant?"

"Go now." There's a definite chill in the air.

I probably should have listened. Should have gone and kept on going, just like Michael. Instead I walk over to my desk to grab my jacket. Which is when the second man emerges from Thacker's office.

This one stoops to make it through the door. He's six-six easy, and that's with bad posture. His dark brown hair is styled in a brush cut with wings in back. His neck is shaved so his ears stick out. He's got a large flat nose and flared nostrils. His eyes are hooded but like two little diamond drills.

The guy looks at me and says, "You want a ride?"

Deep voice, Brooklyn accent.

It's the voice on the phone.

I say no thanks. Thacker and the second man wait for me to leave. There's a distinct whiff of menace in the air.

"I'm going," I say, and do. That is, I hurry down the mezzanine to the Checker and wait by the curb for the big guy to emerge. Three minutes later he comes roaring out of the covered pier in a red Cutlass with rear left fender and trunk lid painted in primer. He heads north along the waterfront then cuts across two lanes to make an illegal U-turn at the next intersection. I do the same. After all, I am a cabdriver.

I follow him south for several miles to an industrial area near the grain elevator. I pull up short one block away as he turns into the lot of Rollaway Trucking, parks in front of the door and goes inside. Forty-five minutes later he hasn't come out.

So I go and make Thacker's delivery.

Sixteen

PAIN.

Not your garden-variety, three-aspirin headache pain. Not your pre-arthritic inflammation of the joints. This is pain that shoots through the foot, up the leg and into my bad knee. Reason is I just stepped on a sharp rock with my bare foot.

"Gina, I'm bleeding."

"There's bandages back in the car."

"I'll never make it. I'm hemorrhaging."

"It doesn't show."

"Oh, thank you. I feel better now. Knowing that it doesn't show."

"Hold still, damn it."

Click.

Here's the situation. I'm posed like a sprinter, left leg and arm straining forward, right leg and arm back. I'm wedged into a crevice in the rock like the last piece of a jigsaw puzzle. The rock is damp and mossy, something's crawling in my left underarm and it's fifty degrees outside. I'm stark naked.

Gina is an art photographer. I mean most of the time she shoots kids who want to be actors, midget egos driven to auditions by their power moms, kids who need head shots to go with their resumés. Occasionally one ends up in a commercial with peanut butter all over his face.

But when Gina shucks off her day job she tramps into the wilderness to be an art photographer. Gina shoots Nudes in Nature. I am the Nude.

Most of the time she doesn't show my face. She crops it out or it's turned away from the camera in a mysterioso pose. I went to the opening of her last show, twenty-five silvery eleven-by-fifteens of my naked body and nobody there knowing who I was. Gina says I look like the Great God Pan with my bare ass peeking through the trees. There's me crammed into the rock, me in the icy mountain stream, me in the splintery abandoned mining shack with stripes of light coming through the cracks like prison bars. Afterwards she dotes on my wounds like Florence Nightingale.

By the way, Gina's good. I'd hang her stuff in my own place only it reminds me of the pain.

"Ouch!"

"Hold still." *Click*.

"I need a break. Union rules."

"You hate unions."

"I love unions. It's work I can't stand. Gina, I am in an advanced state of pain."

"That's important. Wait, I've got to reload."

Eventually I go numb and begin to hallucinate. It's already late in the afternoon because we got lost on the way. Gina wanted to double back to the turnoff but I insisted on going forward. We followed a bumpy dirt fire trail for over an hour until it met back up with the highway. Proving me right again.

A cold breeze kicks up. Gina's wearing a down vest over turtleneck sweater with blue jeans and hiking boots over thermal socks. Her blue black hair tumbles down her back and her olive skin glows in the fading light. I want to kill her.

"By the way," she says without looking up, "got a visit from the cops the other day." *Click.*

I raise my head and smash it into the rock above.

"That's good, Jack, stay like that. Turned out to be a homicide inspector by the name of Lutz. Wanted to know if I knew a guy who got murdered. Somebody from U.S. Customs named Bailey."

"They asked *you*?"

"I'm going, Why would I know somebody like that?"

"What did they say?"

"Said they found my picture in his car."

"*Your* picture?"

"That's what they said. I mean, that's fucking weird, don't you think, Jack?"

"They show you this picture?"

"Yeah. And you know what's funny? Don't move your arm. It's the same fucking picture I gave to you, Jack."

She waits to get me naked and stuffed into a rock before bringing it up. I told you Gina's good.

"Jack?"

I remember now. The picture fell out on the seat of Bailey's car while he was going through my wallet. The cops don't have the wallet but they do have the picture. So why not lift a fingerprint and nail me from the department's print computer? Because I never touched it. Like I said, Gina's the one who slipped it into my wallet. Don't worry, she said, you can always say I'm your sister.

"Oh Jack . . ."

"I'm thinking."

"Fucking right you are."

"I'm trying to remember exactly where I lost that picture."

"You lie to me and I'll leave you out here."

Other photographers' models don't get this abuse. "I can't imagine what you think I'd be doing with a data processing clerk from U.S. Customs."

"You could be anywhere at any time, Jack."

She's right about that. I say, "You tell them it was my copy?"

"Not yet I didn't. Thought I'd talk to you first."

"I remember now it was the whole wallet I lost."

"That makes sense. Customs clerk plays pickpocket in his spare time."

"No, I'm thinking it must of fell out of my jacket that night at Roulette, remember I didn't have any money?"

"You never have any money."

"That's not far from where the guy was killed. He could have found the wallet in a trash can and kept your picture."

"You moved again." *Click.* "I like that image of the guy going through trash cans. Certainly squares with my notion of the U.S. Customs Service."

"Gina, you want the truth?"

"Always, Jack."

"I don't have the slightest idea how your picture fell into the possession of a Customs agent, I mean clerk."

"Let me know if it comes to you."

"Think I could get another copy for my wallet?"

Next day I'm back in the city but sore all over. Gina was silent for most of the way. I guess she suspected I was holding something back. It's around noon on Sunday when she drops me in the Heights and drives off in a huff. From there I go straight to Freddy Fubar's house.

Freddy's a fifty-year-old medical technician who moonlights as the publisher of a punk fanzine. He rents in a lower-middle-class, mixed-use valley surrounded by hills and ritzy homes with panoramic views of downtown and the bay.

The front part of his house is the editorial office of *GIGO*. It's a large carpeted room with a dozen Macintoshes, several laser printers on Formica-topped tables and a layout table. The walls are covered with flyers from punk shows and old covers of *GIGO* but the place is immaculate, not a speck of dust. The monitors are alive with various screen-saver programs, noodly patterns and bouncing balls and flying toasters. Freddy sits at the table in the kitchen off the main room, reading the Sunday funnies and eating a crumpet with butter.

"Fredman."

"Hey, Jack. How's it going?"

He wears his hair in a doo-wop pomp, short on the sides and gone gray at the temples. He's easily thirty years older than the kids who use his house as a crash pad and work on the magazine for room and board, but they get along. Even punkers need a father figure.

"Listen, Fred, you got a guy in your crowd named Michael something or other, bike messenger who wears a dog collar with rhinestones?"

He squints. "Michael, Michael, Michael. Big tall guy with connecting eyebrows. You mean that Michael?"

"I guess. Worked for a while for a guy down at the piers named Thacker. That name ring a bell?"

Freddy shakes his head. "Not especially. I remember Michael, though, blowing through here couple of weeks ago. Left some of his stuff for safekeeping, didn't want anybody messing with it. Wasn't much, couple of bags and some clothes. Stuck it in a closet upstairs."

"Is it still there?"

"He came back and took it all away. Either that or his

girlfriend did, I can't remember. What is it you need him for?"

"Seems he walked off the job one day and disappeared. I want to talk to him about it is all."

"I think he's split. Somebody said something, week or so ago, who the hell was it? Some girl. Anyway, you know these kids. Nobody's tied down to anything."

"I can relate to that."

"Let you know if he turns up, though. Meantime, you want to drop off some papers?" I'm one of Freddy's occasional delivery boys. Stuffing copies of *GIGO* in the free racks all over town, on top of the real estate guides and alternative education catalogs. One step ahead of the newsrack police.

I take an armful of papers and a small stack of CDs beside it. "Okay I take some of these?"

"Go ahead. Write me a review or two." The CDs are bootlegs put out by Freddy, on behalf of bands that have signed with a major label and feel guilty about it.

That's the trouble with kids today. They're too damned principled.

"Jack! Long! time! no! see!"

"Over a week, Maury."

"The! usual?!"

"Beer with a beer chaser." Don't know what he means by "the usual." I never order the same thing twice.

It's Sunday night and the cops still haven't caught on. I'm getting tired of waiting for them to show. Sitting at home was driving me crazy so I got in the Checker and just started cruising around. I even picked up a fare, a drunken businessman at a downtown hotel who made me swear I wouldn't tell his wife. Gave me the idea of coming to the Bilge.

Putz is on lookout at home, he'll call the bar if anything happens. Meantime I can't even talk to Gina, she's still pissed at me about the Bailey thing and her line may be tapped. And tomorrow I go back to schlepping empty packages around town. I'm beginning to think that the cops are doing this to me on purpose. Psychological warfare.

Maury comes back with the beer and slams it down on a Bilge coaster soaked with foam. Next to it he places a new window decal. "Forgot! this! the! other! day!"

"Listen, Maury, has anybody been coming around here asking about me?"

"Anybody! like! who?!"

"Oh, you know, the usual. Cops and the like."

"No! cops! Jack! Well! maybe! just! one!"

Just one. That's a relief. "Uniform or plainclothes?"

"Little! skinny! fellow! Didn't! show! his! badge!"

"What did he ask about?"

"That! dead! guy!"

"The one got murdered last week?"

"That's! the! one!"

"What about him?"

"That! day! he! was! here!"

"What did you tell him?"

"Nothing! Jack!"

"He ask around the bar?"

"Yes!"

"Any names come up?"

"Just! Milo's!"

"How's that?"

"About! how! he! chased! Milo! out! of! the! bar!"

Eight days and the story has become part of Bilge lore. People notice Milo. You want to be invisible, he's the guy to hang with.

"And there was nothing about me?"

"Don't! think! so!"

"Well listen, he comes back, you let me know, okay?"

"He's! here! now! Jack!"

109

"What?"

I look around the bar and see a small man in a suit with dark hair just walking out.

"That's him?"

"That's! him!"

I run for the door, stumble over a bar stool. By the time I get outside the green VW Rabbit is pulling out of the parking lot.

In thirty seconds I'm under way. The Rabbit's half a mile up, doing forty in a twenty-five zone. I close to within a couple of blocks and match his speed. We swing along the pierfronts heading north. I'm about as inconspicuous as a funny car in a funeral procession but the Rabbit doesn't seem to notice. He's just as lousy a tailee as he is a tailer.

He makes a left going away from the waterfront. I squeeze in under a yellow light. We sail along with a block between us like two strangers who happen to be going the same way. The guy can't be using his mirrors. Obviously he never went to traffic school.

He's approaching the tunnel that cuts through the hill and I figure I'd better drop back, he can't be that blind and still be driving. I've just cleared the last light before the tunnel when a diaper service delivery truck pulls out and forces me to hit the brakes. I say something appropriate and swing wide around the truck, so now I'm headed into the tunnel with no way of turning around, as the Rabbit shoots up the little side street just before the tunnel mouth and disappears.

I'm headed in the general direction of home, so I go there.

Seventeen

I CAN'T GET MY MIND OFF the time clock. Not the time clock per se, but Patricia's relationship with it. The clock is over the water cooler in the opposite corner. Patricia's is the only card. Each time she comes or goes she punches the card—*ka-punch*. She holds it with both hands and offers it up like a Fay Wray snack for King Kong. Then she puts it back in the slot with this look on her face like, Have I done the right thing? I think that rubber plant has gone to her head.

Patricia has come back from her coffee break and is dealing with the time clock. She has on a short pleated skirt over tights and leg warmers. I say, "Shouldn't I have one of those?" Referring to the time card.

Patricia gives a start. She freezes with the card in her hands. I've ruined the ritual. I was only trying to be friendly.

"You'll have to ask—"

"Thacker, I know. Listen, that guy on Friday, the Baby Huey type. Does he come around here often?"

Patricia is still holding the card. She looks like a recovering amnesiac. "Yes."

"What are they, partners or something?"

"I don't know. His name is Eddie Fell."

Two consecutive complete sentences. The woman is coming out of her shell. She says, "I think . . . I think they work together."

Yeah, Eddie does all the heavy lifting. "What was that all about on Friday, anyway? Frank and Eddie seemed pissed off at each other for some reason."

"I don't know. They were still arguing after you left."

"You catch any of it?"

She shakes her head, once. Then she shoves the card in the time clock. *Ka-punch*. And mangles the card.

"Oh!" she says.

I've burned through my back issues of *Cab and Cabbie* and am deep into an old copy of *Popular Mechanics* I found wedged into the seat of the Checker. These guys will still be arguing about disc versus drum brakes when they're drooling in wheelchairs. Probably already are.

Round about ten-thirty Thacker comes out of his office. "Mr. Squire," he says.

On my feet. "Yes, sir."

"You were quite a bit delayed coming back on Friday."

"I was?"

"Ninety minutes, to be exact."

"Sorry. My car threw a rod on the hill."

"And now?"

"Now it's fixed."

Thacker gives me a hard look. He stands perfectly balanced, arms loose at his sides. In his hand is a white envelope.

"If it happens again," he says, "I'll find someone else to do the job."

The sixty-second manager. Thacker hands me the envelope. "For Morgenstern," he says, then turns sharply and goes back into the office. He seems depressed, as compared with the jump-for-joy type he was when we first met. Pa-

112

tricia snaps a look at me without breaking stride in her typing. I know better than to ask any more questions.

I get well away from the office before pulling over and opening the envelope. Inside is a copy of the exact same sheet I delivered to Thacker from Morgenstern five days ago, the list of ships and departure dates, only Thacker has made a few changes. He's taken a black felt marker and crossed out all future dates except for the next two. One is tomorrow, the other five days from now.

Plus Thacker has changed that second date, made it one day earlier. He's crossed out DEP and written in ARR. An arrival instead of a departure.

I can picture the argument with Eddie. Thacker's closing up shop and Eddie doesn't like it. The thing with Agent Bailey must have spooked him to the point where he's ready to run. Five more days and it's all over.

It's like a homecoming down at Ingmar Morgenstern & Co., Inc. Richard pumps my hand and says, "Hey, man." Betty gives me a nervous grin, I ask about Howie and she says he's fine. Ted the chess player grunts a greeting. Sigi rises from her desk in surprise. She's wearing an off-white blouse with a ruffled collar under a creamy cardigan sweater so soft I want to rub my cheek against it. Also a tube skirt which shows off her powerful butt muscles.

And there's Ingmar. He comes out of his office and raises his eyebrows with Danish irony. I give him the envelope, hoping to catch his reaction, but he glides back into his office and closes the door.

"So," I say to the room. "Anybody got anything going out?"

Sigi says, "Oh, the computer is fixed."

"Too bad. You free for lunch?"

She gives it some thought. The others pretend they didn't hear anything.

"You pick the place," I say.

"All right," she says.

We take her car. We cross under the freeway to a corner coffee shop which has been there for decades. It has big ceiling fans which go around slowly and dark paneling covered with pictures of the place down through the years. The owners are Italian and treat Sigi like a daughter.

They show us to a table in back. Following Sigi I catch a whiff of her perfume. Something soft and floral. Not at all Teutonic.

It's early still so there aren't a lot of people. The waitress brings us two iced teas without asking. A man in a down vest and gimme cap walks by and Sigi waves. This is her local and she has the edge. Also my back's to the room, which I hate.

I say, "How's Ingmar?"

"I know who you are."

Sigi doesn't go in for small talk. "You do?"

She folds her hands and nods. We're having one of those subtextual conversations but I have no idea what anybody's saying. Your move, Squire.

I say, "You know what strikes me about this business you're in? Everybody seems to be from somewhere else. Why is that, do you think?"

"You know, Ingmar's wife died last year."

"That's too bad. How's his mom doing?"

"Not well. She is getting too old to live alone. He may have to put her in a home."

"And the business?"

"Doing fine. Or was."

She sips her iced tea and looks cool. Underneath she must be a volcano of emotions.

I say, "What is it you think I'm out to do, Sigi?"

"Wreck it." There's a harshness in her voice now, minus

114

the Bavarian singsong. "The whole thing. Without any help from me, by the way."

"You'd never let that happen."

"Don't patronize me. I won't cooperate, no matter what you are promising."

Then it hits me. She thinks I'm a cop.

I do my best to sound like one. "Thing is, Sigi, you may not have a choice. Ingmar either. It'd be a lot better if you both came in."

"Thing is, *Jack*"—Sigi getting sarcastic now—"you don't have a goddamn thing on any of us. If you did, you wouldn't be buying me lunch."

"Actually I was hoping we could go Dutch. The department's pretty tight on expenses."

The waitress comes and we order club sandwiches. I ask for separate checks.

She chats with Sigi for a moment, takes our menus and leaves. I say, "I'm curious about when you figured out who I was."

Sigi smiles for the first time. "You're too smart for a messenger. You ask too many questions."

"Okay, here's one. What if I told you I could get what I needed without hurting Ingmar?"

"I would say you are a liar."

"What if Ingmar was going down anyway?"

"What do you mean?"

I pull out a sheet of paper and toss it over. She stares at it a long time. Finally she says, "What is this?"

"Photocopy of a message I just delivered to Ingmar. Translation: Ingmar's about to lose his best client. I say best because Ingmar strikes me as an honest man who wouldn't be tied up with Thacker if he had a choice. Now Thacker's about to shut down and will probably take you guys with him. Either way Ingmar's mom doesn't have the money for proper convalescent care."

Sigi's still looking at the sheet of paper with the crossed-off sailings. She says, "I don't understand."

"You might if you knew what Thacker's been exporting all this time. And why he's about to turn into an importer."

Sigi says, "Who is Thacker?"

"See what I mean? You'd be so much happier if you knew all the details."

"Bullshit," she says, though without much conviction. She's thinking back, trying to piece it all together in her mind.

I do my best to help. "Try this. Last time you talked about Ingmar losing 'another' container, the one with the Buddhas. When was the first time?"

Sigi thinks some more. "About a month ago," she says. "A container went to Hong Kong."

"Where was it supposed to go?"

"I don't know. Ingmar didn't say."

"The ships on this list all go to Hong Kong."

She glances at the paper. "Among other places. What about it?"

"The ship that's leaving tomorrow night, it goes there too."

"*Ja*, I mean yes. But why?"

"You want to know, check out Ingmar's private records. Look for any mention of Frank Thacker or Eddie Fell or Rollaway Trucking. You find something, call this number." I tear off a strip of paper and write down the number of Putz's private line.

Which snaps her back to reality. "No," she says. "I told you I won't. I must go now."

"Sigi, wait—"

She's halfway to the door already. Then she's gone, leaving behind a cloud of perfume.

116

The waitress brings two club sandwiches. I eat one and ask for the other to be wrapped up. I have both of them put on Sigi's account.

I reach for the sheet of ship departures. Next sailing, tomorrow night at 10 P.M. This must be the last of Thacker's three containers. The first I've got and the second is somewhere in Hong Kong.

I'm going to need a truck.

Eighteen

■■
■■

"JER-*REE*!"

Jerry Mack groans. He rubs his eyes to make me go away. Never works for me either.

"It's just for a few hours, Jer."

I follow him back into his house. Funny thing about Jerry, he never really invites you in. He says, "You ever think about the insurance, Jack? Something happens with you driving the truck? I'm dead, fucking dead."

"I'm a very safe driver. Besides, I've got the hang of it now. Last time was like a practice run."

"But why the hell overnight?"

"It's a scheduling thing. No time to pick it up tomorrow. Look, I'll even throw in some new floor mats."

We're in his living room now. The place definitely needs airing out but Jerry is spiffed up. He's dressed in slacks and button-down shirt, his hair slicked back, and there's an out-of-style checked sport coat hanging over the back of his easy chair.

"Jerry, you look nice, where're you going?"

"To see Melanie and I'm gonna be late."

118

Our mutual parole officer. "Well listen, say hi to her for me."

"I told her I saw you the other day."

"That's cool."

"She finds out you're here again, we're both dead."

"Know what? You ought to listen to your tapes more."

He gets agitated. "You leave off of my tapes!"

"They sort of just tumbled out of the glove box. I promise to leave them alone." Touchy, touchy.

"Anyways I'm takin' off tomorrow night for L.A."

"I'll have it back long before then."

Jerry looks grumpy. He puts on his sports coat and shoots the cuffs. They're an inch too short.

I want him to be happy. I say, "I'll even run it through the car wash for you."

"Just bring it back in one piece." Jerry never actually says yes to anything. He was like that before.

"Simonized, Jer."

I run the truck up from Jerry's neighborhood around eleven o'clock. I'm halfway to the bunker when the green VW Rabbit appears in the big side mirror. I know it's the Rabbit because one headlight is dimmer than the other. Exactly where I picked it up, I have no idea. My mind's been on other things.

I take the next corner at forty miles per hour in high gear. Fortunately I'm not hauling a load. The Rabbit misses the turn and screeches to a halt just past the intersection.

I floor the accelerator on a downgrade as the Rabbit backs up and follows. It's lost about a block. I make a hard right, then an immediate left and shoot down another hill, steeper than the last. No one's behind me and I start thinking I'm clear. Which is when the Rabbit comes tearing out of a side street to the left, half a block back and gaining fast.

I'm no expert in shaking a tail while driving a two-ton

truck. Let alone a souped-up VW Rabbit that's abandoned all pretense of stealth.

Stealth, hell. This is Son of Agent Bailey. I put the pedal to the floor and kick it up to fifty. I still can't find the right gear. My RPMs are in the red and I smell hot brakes or clutch, can't tell which. The Rabbit has closed to within a car's length as I hit the bottom of the hill and open up on level ground.

Level not for long: another hill looms ahead. It's a big one, too, the kind with a sign that says HILL. The light's red at the bottom but I ignore it, I need momentum. Horns blast and tires squeal as I run the light and hit the slope at fifty-five. Right away I'm out of steam and forced to downshift. The Rabbit comes flying up the hill unscathed.

Wrong fucking gear again. I wheeze up the slope with engine screaming, high-speed chase at thirty miles an hour. At the same time I'm swerving to keep the Rabbit from pulling alongside. I'm not going to make the top, I'm already losing control of the truck. Then I think: Why not? Fifty feet from the crest I slip out of gear and take my foot off the brake.

Immediately the truck starts backward down the hill. The Rabbit is too close to swing clear. It has to back straight down just to keep away from me. But I'm picking up speed and the Rabbit can't match me, not while it's in gear. At the last possible moment it veers sharply, glances off the corner of my truck and spins into a driveway.

I barrel on down the hill, out of control. By the time I hit the intersection I'm doing sixty. Thankfully the light is green. Once clear of the intersection I do a frantic three-point turn and take off in a cloud of black smoke. Behind me the light has turned red and trapped the Rabbit on the far side of the street. It's all I need to lose him.

*   *   *

I recover the green container from the bunker without any more trouble. There are unidentified droppings on the ground below the doors, and spider webs in the retaining rods. I chain up the container and haul it to a side street not far from the docks where I left the Checker. My plan is to switch this container with the one Thacker and Fell will be retrieving from the docks tonight. See what's in the other one, stir things up a little, force Thacker to make a mistake.

Before locking the truck I load a few more boxes of Buddhas into the cab. Swear to God I'm going to turn a profit on the damned things.

I get home at a quarter to one. The garage door swings open and I nearly plow into another stack of big white boxes. I blaze a path to the phone.

"Milo!"

"Oh, hello, Jack."

"There are twice as many boxes in my house now, Milo."

"Yes, I think that must be true."

"They're reproducing like rabbits. I nearly broke an ankle."

"Am so sorry, Jack."

"What're you, trying to cut down on your inventory tax?"

"Is nothing like that, Jack. Is very innocent."

"Are we looking at a timetable for removal here?"

"I would say yes."

"Care to share it with me?"

"Is extremely intimate, Jack."

"You mean *imminent*. At least I hope you do."

"Intimate, yes. Is of great help to me, by the way, what you are doing." Milo's English gets worse when he doesn't feel like talking.

"How much you charging for this course, anyway?"

"Excuse me, is the doorbell I am hearing."

I hang up just as I hear a groan. Putz has fallen asleep on my futon in a pile of comic books.

"Oh, hey," he says sleepily. "Milo left those."

"I know Milo left those. I just talked to him."

Putz sits up, suddenly wide awake. "Hey, Jack, check this out, man."

He holds up a comic book encased in a plastic bag.

"What is it, Putz? It's late."

"*Blaster Boy,* man, issue number one. Read it and weep."

I move in for a closer look. Sure enough, it's an immaculate copy of that rare book. And damn good artwork to boot.

"Jesus, Putz. Where'd you get the money to buy this thing? You didn't rip it off from the store, did you?"

"Are you kidding? No way I'd do that, man. No, I hocked one of my old man's silver trays. Broke a window so it'd look like a burglary. You want to read it, gotta wash your hands first."

"Cop was here the other day about that."

"Yeah, the old man was totally pissed. He's freaking out about the security system. He finds out about it, I'm dead. Hey, mind if I keep the book down here for a few days? Just so the maid don't throw it out by mistake."

"Doesn't throw it out. Just stick it on the shelf. Now scram so I can get some sleep."

Thacker stays locked in his office the whole morning. Patricia finishes her typing by nine-thirty and kills the time until lunch by neatening her stack of typed invoices and paging through an office supply catalog. We have a bit of excitement when a deaf guy comes by and tries to sell us some of those wallet-sized cards with the hand signals on it. Patricia improvises her own hand signals to make him go away.

I take my usual lunch hour. Round about two o'clock I

plan to develop a severe case of food poisoning from the hot dog stand out front of the Ferry Building. Then I'll shoot straight out to the docks and swap for Thacker's latest phony shipment. Plenty of latitude in case things go wrong.

I come back from lunch to find Thacker's door open for the first time that day. Eddie Fell sits in the guest chair with his back to the door and Thacker is behind the desk. Eddie's legs are crossed ankle-over-knee and a cigarette dangles from his fingertips. He's way too big for the chair.

Patricia stares at her typewriter. The rubber plant sways in the breeze from an open window. It feels like a Friday, the last day of school, people kicking back. The smell of things wrapping up.

Thacker sees me in the outer office. "Come on in," he says in an almost friendly voice. His windows are shut and the room is full of smoke. So much for spring fever.

A copy of the revised sailing schedule lies open on the desk beside Thacker's Buddha. On the back wall is the framed aerial shot of a big white racing sailboat with rainbow sails. I say, "Nice boat."

"Jack, are you free this afternoon? Nothing to do?" Thacker acting casual, muscular arms behind his head: no sweat stains.

"Actually, I was hoping to take off early for a root canal. My dentist leaves tomorrow for St. Kitt's."

"This won't take long. Will it, Eddie?"

"Nah." Eddie's keeping time to an invisible Walkman. The two of them seem to be getting along again, though I'm convinced they hate each other.

"Good. You can leave with Eddie now."

"Sure you can spare me?"

"He just needs someone to stay with the car. Eddie?"

Eddie nods. Thacker folds the piece of paper and slips it into his desk. I wonder if he left it out for my benefit.

"By the way," I say to Thacker as Eddie prizes himself

123

out of the chair and slings a leather jacket over his shoulder. "You know where I can get one of those Buddhas?"

Thacker looks at the Buddha as if expecting it to speak for itself. He shakes his head. "Cheap novelty item. Sentimental value."

"What're they, made in Hong Kong or something?"

The voice cools off thirty degrees. "I'm not sure."

"You ought to consider selling them, you'd make a mint."

Thacker gives me a look which I charitably interpret as appreciation for my good advice. Eddie stands to the side, cigarette in the corner of his mouth, and motions me through the door. What a gentleman.

We file past Patricia, who's in her usual state of near panic. "Punch me out," I say. Behind me, Eddie grunts.

We take his car, the red Cutlass with the V-8 engine and the very large trunk. The gearshift is thick with rubber bands. On the dashboard is a stick-on plaque from the Sacred Heart Auto League. The car stinks of cigarettes.

We come out of the lot and head north, Eddie humming to himself. Today he's wearing a short-sleeve Hawaiian shirt. His big arms are pink and strangely hairless. A lick of dark hair dangles over his forehead. With one hand he taps a smoke from a pack of Kents and lights it with an old-fashioned Zippo. He snaps the lighter shut and drops it into his shirt pocket. This is when I realize that my window won't go down.

He says, "You mind the smoke?"

"Not a bit." I can choke to death and still keep my hands free. Nobody smokes in my cab. "That Patricia, she's something, huh?"

Grunt. Another strong, silent type. I say, "All that typing she does, she's looking at carpal tunnel syndrome. Nowadays smart employers carry workmen's comp."

"Yak yak yak." Eddie reaches over and turns on an all-news station. Loud.

I talk louder. "Tough finding good secretarial help these days."

Eddie doesn't answer. He drives with his right hand on the wheel at two o'clock, left hand drumming his knee, which is crammed against the dashboard. Even the Cutlass seems too small for him.

He pulls into a white zone alongside the big post office on the edge of the Financial District near the ferry terminal. He reaches under the seat and brings out a handful of manila envelopes. "Wait here," he says. Then he's gone.

We're double-parked beside a row of mail trucks. Eddie has left his flashers on. He's taken the keys and I wonder what I'm supposed to do if a cop or an angry mailman comes along. I can't even play the radio.

Least he could do was leave me a copy of *Penthouse* or *Guns and Ammo*. I look around the floor for something to read. There's a small piece of paper which was dislodged when Eddie pulled out the manila envelopes. It's a receipt for parking at the airport, dated two weeks back. The car stayed there four days. Little vacation for Eddie.

I pocket the receipt. The smoke is making it increasingly difficult to breathe. I reach over and crank the window on Eddie's side. Nothing happens. I shove open both wind wings—you know those old cars still had them—but it doesn't do much good. This is a two-door so the back windows don't roll down at all.

I'm not big on small spaces. Gina wonders how I can stand to live in that garage. Which is a twenty-room mansion compared with a smoke-filled Cutlass whose windows don't open. I wonder if this sort of thing happens with Japanese cars.

I slide over to Eddie's side and pull up on the door handle. It won't budge. The lock button is missing.

I try to remember how Eddie got out of the car. Possibly through sheer strength. I yank the handle again and it snaps off. I throw my body against the door. Good old solid American cars. Built for your basic panzer division.

I stop to catch my breath. My lungs are clogged with cigarette smoke and my shirt is damp with sweat. People are passing on all sides of the car but nobody looks in. I try the glove compartment in hopes of finding a tool or something. Of course it's locked, too.

I'm deciding which window to kick out when Eddie emerges from the post office. He's carrying a package wrapped in brown paper and string. He pauses at the entrance, sucks on a cigarette and squints both ways. Then he flicks the cigarette away and ambles toward the car.

His door opens easily from the outside. Eddie heaves himself onto the seat with a grunt and starts the engine. I don't say anything about his casket on wheels. Somehow I think it's all been said. Message received.

Eddie drops me back at the office and pushes the package toward me. "Boss says deliver this on your way home." He comes around and opens my door from the outside.

Same type package, light as ever, full of air. No questions asked. The address takes me to a row of loading docks not far from Agent Bailey's stakeout point. Around the side is a splintery door with the number 7. There's no obvious place to leave the package. Just as I'm raising a fist to knock on the door, three men converge on me with guns and badges, shove me up against a wall and start patting me down.

"You are under arrest," one of them says, a totally unnecessary piece of information, in my humble opinion.

Nineteen

I'M IN A ROOM WITH WHITEWASHED brick walls and no windows except for the usual one-way mirror, and one small window in the door with safety wire in the glass. And a full blast of fluorescence overhead. Reminds me of my elementary school library.

The table is a thick slab of dark wood on heavy legs with unreadable graffiti gouged in the surface. I wonder what they used for the gouging. I'm sitting on a backless stool across from a pair of folding party chairs. On the tabletop are the two volumes of the Yellow Pages. I won't say anything until I've seen my lawyer.

I feel calm and relaxed but I try not to look it because relaxation's a sign of guilt. And I'm definitely not guilty. We're on the same side, the cops and me. Anyway, what have they got? Not my wallet, we've established that. No prints I can remember leaving. Witnesses, what witnesses? The only person who saw me in that warehouse with Agent Bailey is the one who killed him, and he's not talking.

Clearly I've been set up. Thacker and Fell sending me all over town with empty packages until the right moment.

Which is exactly what I want, the cops playing their hand so I can work up a story. I'm considering the possibilities when the door opens and two cops file in.

The first is a big slow-moving guy with heavy jowls and pouches under his eyes, wirerims on the tip of his nose and a look that says, Let's get this over with and go onto something important, like where we're all going to eat tonight. He's carrying a yellow pad and wearing a baggy gray suit which matches his eyes, a red tie with green diamonds, and gray Hush Puppies. He looks like an English professor.

This'll be Lutz, the one who's been bugging Gina.

"Mr. Squire." Boston accent. Sounds as bored as he looks. "I'm Conklin and that's Appelbaum." Appelbaum gives a stiff little bow. He's taller than Conklin but thirty pounds lighter, with downturned eyelids like quotation marks, downturned mustache and a weak chin which make him look like a walrus about to sneeze. His hair is brushed back but doesn't want to stay that way. He wears an empty shoulder holster over a striped shirt with a mustard stain.

They've already read me my rights and now they do it again. I nod like I understand but don't say anything. Talking to cops while under arrest is Serious Error Number One. In a second I'll ask for my lawyer and the scene will be over.

Conklin lowers his bulk into a folding chair and pulls up to the table with a bad scraping sound. He lays the yellow pad on the table, drops a fresh Bic pen on top of it. "Hell of a system you've got there," he says while Appelbaum nods to himself in the corner. "I'd be curious to know exactly how you move the merchandise. Your method of distribution and all that."

I should say, I want to call my lawyer. Instead I say, "What?"

"Panasonic, Toshiba, JVC, Sony." Conklin says each syllable clearly and slowly. *Pan-a-son-ic, So-nee.* "Finest brands at a fraction of the price, come on down. Ought to advertise on late-night TV."

We're not talking about murder. We're talking about stolen property. They think I've launched a major fencing operation under their noses while still on parole, with extensive *inventory* to boot. How dim can you be?

I say, "Guys, I think you've made a mistake."

Conklin gives a snort. "Hear that, Stan? We've screwed up. We caught a convicted thief at the door of a warehouse crammed floor to ceiling with hot merchandise, and we've made a mistake. Whew, is my face red!"

"Mine too," says Appelbaum.

They're flailing, they haven't got a thing. I play this right, I could be on the street within the hour. Which still gives me time to get down to the piers. It's just after 5 P.M. and the ship doesn't sail until ten.

"Look," I say, "I'm telling you the absolute truth. I don't know a thing about any fencing operation." Appelbaum in the corner gives a little *humph*. "Somebody must have got the address on the package wrong. Post office does it every day."

I tell him about how I'm gainfully employed as a messenger for an exporter down on the piers, guy by the name of Frank Thacker, totally on the up-and-up. I leave out the part about the Buddhas and the rubber plant.

Conklin props his chin on his hand and begins drawing little circles on the yellow pad. "Interesting," he says, and Appelbaum nods. "Considering what was in that package you were delivering."

I say, "What?"

"I think you know. But I want to hear it from you."

I want my lawyer but it would only stretch things out. "I already told you. I'm just a messenger."

Conklin looks surprised. "Of air, Jack? Of fucking *air*?"

I can do surprise, too. Took a few acting classes back in college. "You're saying what, the package was empty?"

"No, you're saying that."

"I'm not saying that."

"That's what I hear you saying. Stan?"

Appelbaum shrugs. "I hear him saying."

"You think I go around opening up packages I'm supposed to deliver?"

Conklin says, "I think the package is bullshit, Jack. I think it's part of a Halloween costume."

"Unh-unh. Nice theory. Totally wrong."

"That's too bad." He looks over his shoulder. "Isn't it, Stan? Man's on parole for possession of stolen property, we arrest him again, and his ass is in a sling. And still he refuses to cooperate. I just don't get it."

Conklin turns back to me but he's still talking to Appelbaum. "I guess I'm just a lousy judge of human nature."

Appelbaum says, "Why's that, Griff?"

"It's like I said. You've got a guy headed back to prison for sure, and us the only people in the world who can help him, and he just sits there with a smartass smirk on his face. It mystifies me, if you want to know."

Appelbaum shrugs again. "Hard to figure."

"It's self-destructive."

I don't take the bait. I figure I'll just play it out, let them run out of steam.

"This Thacker character," Conklin says. "You say he's an exporter. Exporter of what?"

"Whatever. Toys and stuff." Careful here. If the cops spook Thacker he'll close up shop early. Even worse, he gets popped on some penny-ante fencing charge and slides on the murder of Agent Bailey. Like it or not, I've got to protect my boss.

"And stuff," Conklin says. "Like stereos, VCRs, toaster ovens—"

"No way, nothing like that. The warehouse isn't his."

"You know this for a fact?"

"Only from what I've seen. I'm telling you, it's all a big mistake. The guy's legit, as far as I know."

"As far as you know." I hate it when people do that. "You like this man, Jack?"

"What do you mean?"

"Am I not speaking English? Do you like him?"

"Thacker?"

"No, the Dalai Lama."

"Sure I like him."

"Enough to go to prison for him? That much?"

"No."

Conklin raises his eyebrows. "You scared of him?" Over the shoulder to Appelbaum. "I think he's scared of him."

Here I'm supposed to jump out of my chair and say, Nobody scares Jack Squire! and give up the whole operation. "No," I say.

Conklin gives a big sigh. "How old are you, Jack, twenty-four, twenty-five?"

"Twenty-eight."

"That's all right. You come out of prison, you'll still be a young man."

This goes on for another twenty minutes but you get the idea. Finally Conklin's chair scrapes the floor and he stands up. "Let's go, Stan."

Appelbaum gives me a look of disgust as he follows Conklin out of the room. Ten minutes later a cop takes me back to a holding cell. On the way there we pass a clock. It's five minutes to six.

I'm in the holding cell for maybe half an hour. There's a black kid around Putz's age wearing baggy surfer's shorts, tank top and black leather high-tops. He's having an argument with himself. Normally I'd take sides but I'm not in the mood.

Finally the cell door opens and a cop leads me out. I can be down at the piers in twenty minutes. We're headed toward the front desk, where I'll get my stuff back. Then he puts me in another room.

It looks like somebody's temporary office. There's a desk with a blotter and a lamp. Behind it, a counter with a black briefcase.

The cop tells me to sit and wait. Another twenty minutes go by. The chair is soft and springy. A detective peeks in, says he's sorry, and pops out. Outside I hear sirens. I'm just about to check the name on the briefcase when the door opens and Melanie Robinson breezes in.

"So, Jack," she says. "Fucking up again."

"I'm confused. Am I under arrest here, or what?"

She's dressed casually, in khaki pants and a starched blouse. Her perfume is warm and musky. She sits behind the desk. "Just couldn't keep away, could you?"

"It's what I told the cops. I'm an innocent messenger, caught in the grip of a nightmare."

She smiles. "You are much, much stupider than you think."

"I'm working two jobs now, did you hear?" Mr. Personal Initiative.

"You actually think you're fooling people. That's what gets me."

She leans back and rocks in the chair. A minute goes by. I don't dare look at the clock.

I say, "Had a job with a freight forwarder for a while. Gave me a good reference. Which is how I got into this messenger thing. I kind of like it, actually."

She stares at me for another minute or so. Then she takes a file out of her briefcase, opens it up and makes a brief notation. "I'm going to be straight with you, Jack. I'm not going to baby you, or mother you, or give you a pep talk about going straight in the big, bad world. The truth is, I don't give a shit. Not for all the psych texts and work furloughs and halfway houses in the world. Some people just don't take to rehabilitation. People like you, Jack. It's a sure thing you're going back to prison. The only question is when and how fast.

"You've probably figured out that the cops don't have enough to hold you over. You show up at the door of a warehouse full of stolen property with an empty box, so what? If you want my opinion they bungled it, they moved too fast, but that's water under the bridge. The important thing now is to move ahead. I can absolutely guarantee that they're going to nail you, and soon. You weren't smart before and you won't be smart again, it's your nature. And that's just fine by me.

"Here's what you can expect, Jack. You'll be watched every second of the day and night. Nothing you do, nowhere you go, will escape notice. There'll be a cop in your Kleenex box. A cop in your toothpaste tube. And somebody in your underwear drawer. Do we understand each other?"

I can only speak for myself. But no smart cracks. Sincerity is indicated.

"Yes, ma'am," I say.

"Good." She slips the file into her briefcase and latches it. "See you soon, Jack."

She stalks out of the room. I must have interrupted her dinner. The clock says ten to eight.

Nobody has said I can go. I try the door, which is locked. I wait fifteen minutes but nobody comes. They must have forgotten about me. I knock on the door, softly at first, then harder. Then I start to yell. I hate being cooped up.

At eight-twenty a cop unlocks the door like nothing unusual has happened and leads me to the front desk where

133

I get my things back in a Ziploc bag with SQUIRE written on masking tape. I sign a form and I'm back on the street. No time to waste, I'll have to catch a cab.

There isn't a cab in sight.

Twenty

■■
■■

I WALK SIX BLOCKS BEFORE finding a cab to take me down to
Jerry Mack's truck. It's a clear warm night with hardly any
wind. A few people are wandering around but nobody's
paying any attention to me. Before climbing into the truck
I scope the area for a green Rabbit, or an unmarked police
unit, or Eddie Fell's Cutlass, or anybody else who has nothing better to do than follow me around. Zip on all counts.
Gentlemen, start your engines.

By the time I reach the piers it's five past nine. Chances
are Eddie Fell has come and gone but I figure it's worth a
try anyway. I'm about to drive up to the terminal gate when
I see a truck already parked at the gatehouse that says
ROLLAWAY TRUCKING on the side, hauling an empty chassis.
Missed it by minutes.

The Rollaway truck disappears into the terminal. What
the hell, I think. I'm too late to switch the containers, maybe
I can steal them both. Wouldn't that really piss Thacker off?
I park Jerry's truck and cross the street on foot.

"Evening," I say to the gatehouse guard.

"Evening." He's reading a copy of *TV Guide*. Each to his

135

own. I hand over a sheaf of papers. My brief interlude at Ingmar Morgenstern & Co., Inc. has taught me all about the documents I need to get in.

"I'm with Rollaway," I say. "Driver forgot this stuff."

The guard waves me through with scarcely a look. I'm standing in the middle of empty tarmac with a big containership looming off to the right, all lit up. It looks like a skyscraper lying on its side. The cranes are quiet and the ship's ready to sail. Nearby is a white, two-story building with the insignia of the U.S. Customs Service on the door. I go left, in the direction the Rollaway truck went.

I jog toward a five-high stack of containers in the opposite corner of the yard. There's a truck parked nearby but I can't make out its colors. Everything is orange under the yard lights. I take the long way round the stack, creep along several rows and peer out to see Eddie Fell, talking to a man in a hard hat and reflecting vest beside a small top-lifter on wheels. He's tapping a piece of paper and the man is nodding.

I duck back behind the stack of boxes and keep circling around. I move quickly from row to row, and now I'm thirty yards from Eddie's truck. I watch the top-lifter move a container from stack to chassis. Eddie is nowhere to be seen.

Between me and the truck lies open space. I can't get any closer under cover. The driver's side door hangs open and the motor is idling. I can even see the keys dangling from the ignition. I'm about to seize the moment when somebody delivers a wallop to the side of my head with what feels and sounds like a sack of marbles. I see a bright flash and crumple to the ground like a sack of dirty laundry. That's all I know for a while.

When I wake up it's pitch dark and my head hurts so bad it's like somebody stuck my head in a subwoofer and blasted the Dukes of Pus, who I normally like. I'm surrounded by boxes, and moving. My head throbs in time with the intermittent horn of a truck backing up. It's the horn on Jerry Mack's truck. I try getting up but lose my grip and fall back on somebody who screams in pain.

Actually it's a Buddha, several of them, judging from the sound. I'm trapped in my own container, in the small space left by the cartons I took out. We hit a bump and a box lands on my head. I don't know why we're backing up but I wish somebody would turn off that goddamn horn. I grope for the doors, which are locked, so I start banging away with my fist. No response. The container keeps on moving.

I don't have a lot of room to maneuver, maybe ten feet square. A stack of boxes nudges me and I shove it back into place. I yell again but I know it's hopeless. I'm in here for a reason.

The truck engine revs and we start picking up speed. We're going five, maybe ten miles an hour. Underneath is a rhythmic bumping, like we're going over planks. Then the truck lurches to a stop and a whole pile of boxes rains down on my head. The edge of one catches me in the neck and I go crashing into a pile of Buddhas. Colors swim around me like deep-sea fish. I black out again.

When I come to I hear the sound of chains on wood, then a minute or so of silence and the slamming of a truck door. I yell as loud as I can but my voice is deadened by cardboard. I'm pinned down by a pile of boxes. I try to move and a Buddha screams.

We're moving again, creeping along at two or three miles an hour. Why so slow? Somebody's got to notice us and wonder what the hell is up. Goddamn truck is right there in the middle of the terminal. At least it was.

I try yelling again but nothing comes out. Suddenly the container tips downward and the entire load shifts and pins me against the doors so I can't breathe. There's a terrible scraping sound and a big splash. The container's going end over end and I can't tell up from down. Water is rushing in.

For a second I think the doors have broken open, but they're sealed tight. I have no idea where the water is coming from. All I know is, I'm under it and the container is filling up fast.

The boxes must have shifted again because I have a little room to maneuver. Everywhere I step a Buddha screams. The water is already up to my neck. I climb a box and find a fast-shrinking pocket of air. I'm going strictly by sense of touch. My head bumps against the ceiling as water runs into my nose and mouth.

My head goes under and I'm out of air. Even underwater I can make out the muffled scream of a Buddha. Or maybe it's my own screams I hear.

My body wants to give up but my brain is still functioning. It's telling me something I don't want to hear, for some reason in the voice of Peter Lorre. It's saying, *Stupid idiot! Don't avoid the water! Go toward it!* Which I take to be the onset of delirium until I realize that the water must be pouring through a hole, and the hole might be big enough to get through. Assuming I have any air left in my lungs.

I've lost all sense of direction but I go where I think the water's coming from, in a corner of the ceiling which used to be the floor, or maybe the other way around. No matter, it's the place where the container scraped the edge of the pier and was ripped open to let the water in. I stumble over boxes full of Buddhas which are starting to float and becoming easier to push aside. My lungs are in agony and all I can feel is a wall of corrugated metal. It's like somebody has me in a great big fist and is squeezing the life out of me.

My hand snags on something sharp. It's the jagged edge of a hole, can't tell how big. I try shoving my body through. My shirt catches on the edge, which is bent inward. I tear at it frantically and the shirt rips off my body. I grab both edges and launch myself through the hole. At the last moment my foot gets caught. I kick off my shoe and black out.

Cold air brings me back. I'm bobbing in the bay, not far from a crumbling pier. Beyond it, a forest of city lights. Overhead the bridge looms. Swells keep washing over me and I have to dog-paddle to stay afloat. My arms feel like diver's weights and my lungs are on fire. Slowly I push my way toward the shore. With every third stroke I'm driven underwater. Each time it gets harder to come up.

I'm barely conscious but I manage to aim for a dinghy tied to a concrete block sunk into the ground. Low tide. I flop ashore in a state of pain and undress. I look like Bruce Banner after changing back from the Incredible Hulk. Makes posing for Gina seem like snoozing on silk.

I beach myself on the gravel for a while, forcing up gobs of seawater and bile. My lungs are calming down but my arm is bleeding heavily. Even so it's my neck and back that hurt the most. Always been my weakest points.

One of these days I've got to look into getting some workmen's comp.

Twenty-one

■■
■■

I GO TO GINA'S APARTMENT, never mind the mysterious Detective Lutz. I'm in need of an expert in field dressings.

I make it up three of the four flights and collapse on the stairs. I imagine her bitching about the blood on her pale blue gray carpet. I decide I like it there and resolve not to move till morning.

"Oh my God!" Gina comes running down the final flight of stairs. "God, Jack!"

"Don't move me," I say. "This is nice."

"Stay there," she says, as if I'd been threatening to move. "I'm calling an ambulance."

I manage to raise my voice above a whisper. "No," I say as a door on the floor below opens. "Just help me get inside."

She gets behind me and slips her arms under my armpits. Somehow she helps me to my feet and drapes my arm around her shoulder. We stagger up the steps like wounded buddies in a World War II movie.

"God, Jack," she says, straining under my weight. "What the fuck happened to you?"

"I found a photographer even tougher than you."

Her place is immaculate, as always. The plants are watered and her books are alphabetized. Her morning paper is folded up neatly on the coffee table with the sections in order. If Gina were blind, she'd be able to find everything.

"So. Jack."

Explanation time. It's twenty minutes later and I'm sitting on her love seat, my arm bandaged up and an ice bag on my head, which feels fine if I don't move my eyes. Actually I'm not as bad off as I first appeared to be.

Gina stands across the room with her arms crossed, street light glowing in her hair. She seems afraid to get too close.

"Had a run-in with a bad tourist," I mumble. "Got to stop picking up tourists. Fucking Elks and Lions'll take your head off."

She looks out the window and down to the sidewalk. "That Jerry's truck you're driving?"

"He needed my cab for the night. Guess he wanted to impress some girl."

Then I think, Jerry's truck. It was Jerry's truck that backed me into the bay, not Eddie's Rollaway rig, with me inside that first container full of Buddhas, the one I found on Pier Street. Which is why the boxes were slipping around, because I had taken some of them out. I found the truck minus chassis at the edge of the pier with the keys in the ignition.

Doesn't make sense, I think groggily as Gina drones on in the background. Why would Eddie sacrifice one of Thacker's three containers?

"Jack!"

"What?"

"I said, Have the cops been to see you yet?"

My head throbs. "You mean about that picture thing? Nobody's asked me about that. No reason to." I don't like lying to Gina, it isn't healthy. Sometimes I do it anyway.

"You are one lucky fucker, Jack."

Let her think that. All I know is, I'm suddenly starving. "You know what? I could use a peanut butter and jelly sandwich or something. Haven't eaten all day."

Gina looks at me suspiciously but goes into her kitchenette to make the sandwich. She'd do it even if my arm was okay, but she'd bitch like hell about it. Now she doesn't say anything. It makes me nervous.

It's after midnight and the skyscrapers are dark except for the floors where the janitors are at work. A car goes by in the alley below, kids yelling. I say, "You mind if I stay over tonight?"

"If you want," she says.

"Good, 'cause I don't feel like driving home." Which is a pain, since Gina won't even let me keep a toothbrush at her place. I'll have to use my finger.

She says, "Won't Jerry miss his truck?"

"No, he let me have it for the night."

Gina slaps the sandwich on a plate and brings it over. She's put a few Pretzel Goldfish on the side. She feels my forehead with a cool palm. "Sorry your mom's not around to do this."

"You make the best peanut butter sandwiches."

"Ever feel like learning, just let me know."

Sarcasm. Gina hates it that I don't know how to cook. I say, "Eventually I'd like another bottle of aspirin. Don't get up now."

"You want me to change your fucking diaper, too?"

Right away she looks sorry she said it. I let it go. I say, "I'm thinking of calling Putz, have him bring over some clothes."

"Whatever."

"He'll be happy to come over. He likes you, you know. We're talking big-time crush."

She picks up a Pretzel Goldfish that slipped off my plate.

142

"What worries me is he likes *you*. You're a bad influence on a kid that age."

"I'm a bad influence all round," I say, meaning it as a joke, but Gina doesn't laugh.

"Come on, Jack. A boy like that needs a role model, somebody to look up to," she says. "Instead he gets somebody with an emotional age of ten."

"Don't knock ten. It was a very good year."

But Gina has gone silent. She's in no mood for snappy patter. I try another tack. "Listen, babe, you free this weekend? I was thinking maybe we could get up north to a B & B."

She's caught off guard. "This weekend? I'll have to check." Normally she'd say something like, A whole fucking weekend? You sure you want to commit for that long?

"No big deal," I say. "Spur-of-the-moment thing."

"Jack, are you all right?"

Gina's standing over me now. There's genuine concern in her face. She's been circling the room, getting closer and closer. Now it's Heavy Talk time. I say, "What do you mean?"

"I'm having this sick kind of feeling. About you and this Bailey guy. I'm afraid you've finally gone too far. Tell me straight out it isn't true."

Agent Bailey, the Lone Avenger. It's been nine days and I'm no closer to clearing his name, let alone nailing his killer. I haven't even managed to sell a single Buddha.

"You know," I say, trying to stretch, "maybe the arm's not so bad after all."

"Jack . . ."

I try standing up. The room starts to swim and I settle back into the love seat. Gina sits beside me, her hand on my thigh.

"Tell me, Jack."

I say, "I really ought to go."

"What!"

"Some things I ought to be doing. I'll be all right. And no, it isn't true about Bailey."

"Fuck Bailey. Why is it that every time I'm halfway nice to you, every time I want to talk, you take off?"

I feel the urge to move but my body vetoes it. My car keys are on the bar, out of reach.

"I'm talking to you, Jack."

I pretend to pass out.

Gina groans. "I am such a fucking idiot."

I don't wake up to argue the point.

Twenty-two

"MORNING, PATRICIA."

I've brought her a hot cinnamon roll with icing, fresh squeezed orange juice, and a long-stemmed rose in green paper. Patricia looks at the rose as if it were crawling across the desk. Maybe the problem goes beyond the rubber plant.

Now she's staring at me. My arm is bandaged and there's a good-sized bruise on my forehead. I don't feel so bad after a night's sleep.

"It's all right," I say. "Had a little run-in with a bike messenger yesterday. Thacker here yet?"

"Unh-unh."

I didn't think so. It's five to nine and he doesn't usually show until quarter past. I want to see his face when he walks through the door. I'm working up a theory.

Patricia stares at the rose. "I don't have a vase," she says. Pronouncing it *vahz.*

"No problem. Florist threw in one of those little water vials. Last you till lunchtime."

"Thank you."

"Don't mention it."

145

"I got you a card."

"What?" I wonder if she thinks it's my birthday or something. But it's a blank time card she's holding out.

"Hey, thanks," I say. "We'll call it an even swap." I bear the card over to the time clock with suitable formality. "Like this?"

"I'll show you." She comes over and takes the card from my hand. She holds it over the jaws of the clock. Then she jams it into the slot. The clock goes *ka-chunk* and she recoils with the card still in her hand. Safe again.

She hands the card back. The time is stamped in bright red ink. I never had to punch a time clock before. "Wow," I say. "I feel like I finally belong."

"I don't."

Cue motivational speech. " 'Course you do. You're like part of the furniture here. Without you, Thacker'd be—"

"It's my last day."

"No!"

"Frank says there's nothing left for me to do here."

"How can that be, all that typing—"

"Finished. So he says."

"Well, . . . what's he going to do?"

She looks at me funny. Wrong question.

"I mean you, Patricia, what are *you* going to do?"

"Go back to the agency. Only this was the first job where I was able to work for more than a day. Even though it had . . ."

"Had what, Patricia?"

Dread crosses her face. I can't hear what she's saying.

"What was that?"

Still only a whisper. "Plants."

"*Plants?*"

She nods. "I can't handle . . . plants."

"Like that rubber plant there?"

146

She shudders. "Yes."

"You mean you're allergic."

"No. I'm phobic."

"Where do you think it comes from?"

"I don't know. Once when I was about three, I saw this movie about plants that walked? Maybe that was it."

"Shit, and I gave you a rose."

"That's okay. I was the one put the rubber plant in my corner. It used to be way across the room."

"Why'd you do that?"

"The agency said they couldn't keep me on if I couldn't work around plants. Ever seen an office without plants?"

"I admit, it does seem to be the thing these days."

"So I decided I'd better get used to it."

What a trooper. "Thacker give you a recommendation?" She shakes her head.

"Yeah he did." I pick up one of the blank invoices. "We'll stat this letterhead onto a blank piece of paper. I'll say you're the best secretary in the Free World."

Patricia blushes. Hell of a girl. Marshmallow on the outside, Almond Roca on the inside. The outer door opens and Thacker walks in, ten minutes early.

I brace for a reaction, the momentary look of shock when he sees me alive. You can't cover up in those first few seconds.

He grunts at Patricia, then at me, and goes into his office.

I follow him in and close the door. Thacker's standing by the window in khakis and tight polo shirt, looking at the bay. Probably dreaming he's out there sailing, all tanned and glistening with seaspray. Whatever Eddie Fell is up to, he doesn't know about it. Which is why Eddie dumped the container in the bay, with me inside.

I'm in the mood to bust his bubble. I say, "Got arrested yesterday afternoon."

He raises his eyebrows. "Excuse me?"

"That address you sent me to? Turned out to be a warehouse full of hot merchandise."

Thacker sits down and starts fiddling with some papers. I can tell they're from his safe. "Then it was a mistake."

"That's what I told the cops. Said you had nothing to do with it. Of course they wondered about the package."

The fiddling stops. "They opened it?"

I nod.

"And what did you tell them?"

"That it was another mistake. Big royal fuck-up all round."

He's thinking hard. I'm figuring to let him sweat for a moment.

Finally I say, "Luckily they didn't ask about the other packages."

His eyes go cold. "You opened them?"

"It's compulsive behavior. I'm working on it."

"That was none of your damned business."

"It's all right, I don't mind being a decoy. Throw the cops off the trail while you're off doing what you're doing. I'm willing to bet you didn't even know that warehouse was full of hot goods. I ever tell you, I'm on parole?"

Now he's really thinking. I can almost see the steam coming out of his ears. "For what?"

"Random larceny and mayhem. It's the reason they gave me so much shit. Eventually they had to let me go. 'Course I'm a prime candidate for getting picked up again. Guys like me have got to watch our step all the time."

He nods slowly, like I'm proving a point.

"By the way, Ingmar thinks you sent me to him in the first place. Just like you thought he sent me to you. Actually I just showed up at his place one day on a whim. I was planning to rob him blind."

Thacker turns away from the window and speaks in a near whisper. "What do you want?"

"Want? *Moi?* To work for you. Best job I've had in years."

His eyes are pale, even dead. "Well, let me tell you something, Mr. Squire. I don't take well to people crossing me, not for an instant. I don't tolerate blackmail or disloyalty or even smart-mouth cracks. You try it and I'll have your head, just like that, do you understand?" He snaps his fingers on the word *just*.

"Absolutely. Sir."

"Now. Got anything else to tell me?" His voice is different now. There's a touch of the street in it, maybe even a Brooklyn accent. The boaty voice is a front.

"Only that Patricia got me a time card."

Thacker doesn't have time to react. There's a knock at the door and Eddie Fell comes in.

He says, "I need to borrow the kid."

Eddie hulks over the two of us. Thacker looks at him strangely. For a second I could swear there's fear in those pale eyes. Then he says to Eddie, "Be my guest."

The Cutlass is parked in a red zone outside the pier. Eddie floors it. Those old V-8s, they used to make them big. One-third engine and one-third trunk.

I had a choice not to get in. There's nothing Eddie could do in public. But something in my stomach tells me to go for it. I can talk to him, I think. I can work both ends. There's no other way.

Too late to turn back now. I say, "Thacker told me about that container you lost. Hope you had insurance."

"Shut your fucking mouth."

It's a start. The light goes yellow and Eddie slams on the brakes. I wish he hadn't, there's a patrol car at the corner.

The cops are drinking out of Styrofoam cups and eating croissants. Eddie drums his fingers on the steering wheel and bounces his knee. The man can't sit still. Finally the light turns green and Eddie guns the engine. The cops pay no attention.

"I'm serious, Eddie, those Buddhas cost like seventy bucks apiece retail. Figure four thousand or so in that one container, plus the container itself, it adds up to some real money for a small-time exporter like Thacker. Think he's got the cash to replace it?"

The fist connects with my jaw and smashes my head against the window. Rabbit punch. Hard to believe the glass didn't break. My head hurts on both sides.

"By the way, that was one hell of a setup yesterday," I say. "I walked right into it."

"I said shut the fuck up," Eddie says.

I move my jaw to make sure it's not dislocated. Already it's beginning to throb horribly. The plan isn't exactly working out. I decide not to say anything more till we get to where we're going.

Which is a mile away in an alley near the piers on the northern waterfront. Eddie has a thing for places near water. He blocks the alley with the Cutlass and opens my door. He drags me out and frog-marches me down the alley, which ends in a pile of trash and a high wall with a ventilator grille twelve feet over my head. I can see the blades of a big fan revolving inside it. Time to improvise.

"Eddie." He's backing me toward the trash. "Let's make a deal."

He pulls out a switchblade. "Turn around, punk."

I scan the trash heap for some kind of a weapon. It's nothing but scraps of cardboard, all black and sticky with tar.

I say, "You notice I haven't told Thacker you've gone independent?"

"The fuck does that mean?"

The parking receipt in Eddie's car. The container that wasn't supposed to go to Hong Kong. "Your little trip to Hong Kong to work out the details. Probably told Thacker you had food poisoning for four days. Now you're afraid I'm going to blow apart the whole thing."

"I ain't afraid of you, you little piece of shit. Now turn around."

"I could have told him about you this morning, but I didn't."

"So fucking what?"

"So I can stop him from closing up shop. You're aware he's about to do that? He's not even going to wait for the last shipment, Eddie. He's terrified the cops are about to bust him but I can talk him down. It's me they want, not him, he's just running scared. Your whole plan's going to collapse, just like that. Plus I've got connections, I can move the merchandise for you, it's what I do. I'm your classic middleman, I never touch the stuff. Ask any cop, Eddie—"

He shoves me in the chest and I fall backward into the pile of trash. Even the stupidest guys I can usually talk to. Eddie reaches for me, grabs me by the shirtfront, swings me around. I'm trying to angle for a good kick in the balls. Now he has one arm tight around my throat. In the corner of my eye I see the glint of the knife. It's arcing toward me when Eddie goes *oof* and I fall to my knees. There's the sound of another blow and Eddie flies right over me into the trash heap. Somebody shoves me aside and goes for him.

I look up to see a little guy in a navy blue suit, five-five or -six and 150 pounds, whaling away at the Eddie the Lug. Every time Eddie raises his arms to fend off the blows, the guy slugs him in the stomach. Then the arms come down and Eddie gets it in the face. If only he could get up, he might put up a fight. But the little guy has the element of surprise, and now Eddie is stuck in the cardboard and can't get any leverage.

A few more punches and Eddie's quiet. He's not unconscious but he's breathing hard and bleeding from his nose and right eye, arms outstretched in the tar-covered trash. The assailant backs off and brushes down his cheap suit. A shock of black hair dangles over his forehead and his knuckles are scraped raw.

"How did you do that?" I ask him.

"Never mind." He holds out a hand. "Let's get out of here before he comes to his senses."

Twenty-three

■■
■■

HE'S YOUNGER THAN ME or looks it, twenty-five tops. Maybe it's the hair flopping in his eyes, or the button nose, or the voice like a teenager's. Boyish is the word. He's Junior G-Man. We're driving along the waterfront in his dark green VW Rabbit.

Everything looks unusually clear and sharp. I have my window wide open. "You are one persistent whatever-you-are," I say.

"You're pretty persistent yourself."

Miller Time. "Mind telling me what it is you do for a living?"

Without taking his eyes off the road he reaches into his jacket and tosses over a black vinyl badge holder. I've seen one before.

"U.S. Customs Service," I read aloud. "Inspector Paul E. DeMarco."

"Just Paul is fine." He holds out his hand for the badge. Like I was going to keep it. I get the eerie feeling this guy really knows me.

I say, "I guess you knew Agent Bailey."

"Ray was no agent. But yeah, I knew him."

"And you think I killed him."

"I did for a while. Not anymore."

"May I ask what changed your mind?"

"Lots of things. Basically, you're too small-time to do anything like that."

"Thank you very much."

"Don't mention it."

When he's not following anybody, Inspector DeMarco drives carefully. He stops for old ladies in crosswalks and yields the right of way at intersections. His Rabbit is buffed and vacuumed and in pretty good shape even though all VWs smell alike. I'm betting the ashtray is totally buttless. Behind his seat is an Adidas bag with a dirty shoelace sticking out of it.

I say, "You work out?"

"Five times a week at the Y. Mostly swimming and free weights."

"Some boxing, too?"

He shrugs. "It comes."

"So what was he doing in that warehouse? Bailey, I mean."

"Proving himself."

"Know something?" I say. "Agent or no agent, the guy was good."

"I know that. You know that. But it didn't matter to the U.S. Customs Service."

"The paper said Bailey had a record."

"That's right. Boosted a couple of cars twenty years ago, smoked a little weed, did eighteen months in the joint. Those kind of mistakes stick like Krazy Glue, you can't get bonded."

"I've heard that."

"We worked at the pier together so I got to know him a

little. All he ever wanted was to be a cop. He hung out in cop bars every night, even had a police radio in his car. Told me he worked for two weeks once as a security guard at an auto impound. It was a comedown, but a little like being a cop. Anyway, the boss found out about his record, kicked his butt over the chain-link fence. Then he comes to Customs, and all he can get is input clerk."

"Which is how he latched onto Frank Thacker."

"That's right," DeMarco says. "I figure he found something off-pace in the broker filings and decided to run it down all by himself. Input clerks are the first to see any red flags."

"Too bad he didn't tell anybody about it."

"Guess he decided to play cowboy. He had a few weeks before the shipment actually came in. Thought Customs would be so grateful they'd make him a full-fledged inspector. No chance of that happening."

"So what do you think he found out?"

"Like I said, about a suspect shipment."

"From Hong Kong," I say. "Arriving in three days."

DeMarco looks at me. "What do you know about that?"

"I know it's Thacker's first stab at being an importer. Only he may not know what he's really importing."

"Do you?"

I shake my head, which hurts. "What I hear is, the container got away from him by mistake. It wasn't supposed to go anywhere. Now it's coming home."

DeMarco nods like this is common knowledge. What he really knows, he isn't telling.

I say, "So you're planning to nail both Thacker and Fell?"

"For the shipment, that'll be easy."

"But you want more."

"Uh-huh."

"You want them for the murder of Agent Bailey."

155

"That's right."

My man. It's personal with him, too. "And the way you're going to do that is . . . ?"

"Through you."

DeMarco has skirted the big hill to our left and is headed toward the Heights, where I live. My head is throbbing. I wonder if I've got enough hot frequent-flier coupons for a trip to Tierra del Fuego.

"You're taking me home?" I say.

"If that's where you want to go. We'll meet tomorrow at your bar. Talk about our next step."

"Actually, I'd like to pick up my cab. It's in the other direction, back near Thacker's office."

DeMarco does a U-turn in the middle of the block, narrowly avoiding a bus. That's more like him.

"For what it's worth," I say, "I think it was Fell, the guy you left back there in the alley, who actually killed Bailey. Thacker may have found out later and that's why he's closing down the operation."

"Doesn't matter. He's an accessory. So you're in?"

I feel my swollen jaw, the sting in my arm. It's the perfect moment to back out, let the professionals handle it.

"I'm in," I say.

It's nice having the Checker back. She's a little dirty from having sat out all night, so I run her through the car wash. I even spring for the air freshener, Evening Everglade. Smell it? It's like driving around inside a tree.

I do a quick tour of the city, the scenic route, up and over the hills from ocean to bay. I can't account for this pumped-up feeling until I realize I'm jazzed just to be alive. Delayed reaction from the last twelve hours, I guess. Nothing like an occasional brush with death to open up your sinuses. Beats the hell out of taking drugs.

I stop back home for a sponge bath and a change of

bandages. Still no cops and I'm beginning to think there won't be. I put on my light brown cords and deep blue Hawaiian shirt with the red hibiscus. Then it's back down the peninsula to Ingmar Morgenstern & Co., Inc.

Something's different about the office today, something slightly off. Betty's sitting at reception doing her nails. The others are working away but it's too quiet, nobody talking or panicking or rushing around. Like something happened just before I came through the door.

Sigi's wearing a soft green jumper, white turtleneck underneath, and fuzzy white tights. It's a different look for her, but it works. She and Ingmar are just coming out of his office.

Both of them look at me with open hostility. Closing ranks against the enemy.

"Jack," Sigi says.

"Ingmar, can you spare Sigi? I want to take her to lunch."

Sigi smolders. "I'm in the room, Jack."

Ingmar says, "You have something for me? A message, perhaps?"

"Nope. Nothing but a social call. I kind of missed the old place."

Ingmar stretches his neck and returns to his office to work on his audition for the part of Death in the road show of *The Seventh Seal*. The others let out their breath. Work resumes.

Sigi says, "I'm very busy today."

"No prob. We'll have a short lunch, across the street."

Sigi's place. But I march in there like it's mine. I say hi to the owner at the register, shake his hand and talk a little baseball. He shows us to the same table, the only one that's left.

The waitress greets us like old friends, calls me Hon and puts down two iced teas. She hands us menus and leaves us alone.

Sigi hasn't said a word. She's fuming.

I say, "I like this place. There's a family kind of feel to it. How's their Sunday brunch?"

"I know what you're doing, Jack, walking into the office like that to scare me into cooperating. It's not going to work. What do you want, anyway?"

"It's down to either a BLT or a club. Can't make up my mind."

"That is not what I meant."

"What's up over at Morgenstern's? Everybody's walking around like somebody died."

Sigi sips her iced tea.

"Okay," I say, putting on my cop attitude, "here it goes. The Buddhas? Forget about the Buddhas. This is about a murder now. You remember that guy got wasted down on Pier Street couple of weeks back? Right across the street from Thacker's warehouse? Well, U.S. Customs is involved now. I've met the guy, he's nice, but he's tough and won't take any crap. You want to keep Ingmar free and clear, you'll cooperate with me and that's that."

"Today Ingmar told me he wants to quit."

"Bosses can't quit. It's like your parents running away."

"He says retiring but it's quitting he means. He wants to shut down everything. All of us will be out of a job."

"I've been trying to tell you, Sigi, it's Thacker who's quitting. Ingmar's silent partner. He's the one about to pull the rug out from under."

Sigi's not listening. "Ingmar has a lot on his mind. His mother isn't well. He hasn't been at work much. He's afraid he's going to jail."

"Didn't I tell you I can keep him out?" Maybe, maybe not. But I like making people feel good.

"And what do you want from me?" Looking at me now, looking scared.

I show her the list of ship departures. "Find out about this shipment coming in on Saturday. Why they're calling it an arrival instead of a departure. What's supposed to be inside."

Sigi scans the paper. "He has a place for his private files."

"Then go for it. Call me up when you know."

We stick with the iced teas so Sigi can get back to work. After she's gone I sit for a while and think things through. I may have to divert that incoming container if we can't make the murder rap stick by Saturday. Can't have Thacker and Fell going down for something trivial.

Then I have one of my little brainstorms. Maybe, I think, maybe I'll divert that container anyway.

Twenty-four

■■
■■

DETECTIVE STAN APPELBAUM IS MY uninvited houseguest, his car parked in front of my open garage. He's lucky I didn't run him down from force of habit. I'm getting more careful about that.

Appelbaum stands in front of my shelves like he's in a lending library. He's two feet from the picture of Agent Bailey's family but doesn't notice it. Instead he's rifling through a stack of comic books. He pulls out an old *American Flagg*. It's a classic ish, in comic book lingo. He fans the pages.

"Careful," I say. "Too much handling cuts down on its value."

"Don't get bent out of shape. I've got a warrant."

I hadn't sounded bent out of shape. He tosses the comic away and runs a finger along my shelves like he's checking for dust. Amazing what's a crime these days.

Appelbaum turns slowly around with hands on hips. He's wearing a shiny blue double-breasted suit with the jacket unbuttoned. There are coffee stains on his tie.

"Heard a funny thing today," he says. "Report of a burglary right here about a week ago. Owner lost a priceless silver tray."

"I heard that."

"How much did you get for it, Jack? Fifty, sixty bucks? What happen, you run out of mad money and Daddy wouldn't give you any more allowance?"

"You're flailing, Stan."

"Am I? I doubt that."

"You never saw *Les Misérables?*"

"What the fuck are you talking about?"

"People change, Stan. It's a wonderful thing to behold."

"All I know is, if I was a millionaire, I wouldn't let some scum stay in my garage. Although money does funny things to some folks. Makes 'em soft, I guess."

"You want to look around, you're welcome to it."

"I don't need an invitation." He starts wandering slowly around the room. He opens all the drawers, paws through my T-shirt collection, pushes aside Putz's rare issue of *Blaster Boy* in protective plastic. He examines Mr. Machine and the Creature From the Black Lagoon, which took me three hours to paint. He places a tentative foot on the hydraulic lift. He's peering in at the three dozen burritos in my miniature freezer when Putz walks in.

"Hey, Jack, I—" He stops short.

"It's okay, Putz. This is Lieutenant Appelbaum of the Burglary detail. I think he's going to have a burrito. Lieutenant, this is McAllister Huffington, son of the man you were just talking about."

"Hi," Putz says through a wad of bubblegum, and flops down on the futon to play Attack of the Plasmoid People II.

Appelbaum gives a look of disgust. "Real fine influence," he says.

I say, "Putz, I mean McAllister, comes down here from time to time to kick back. It's sort of his—"

"Sanctum sanctorum," Putz says.

"That's right, his sanctum sanctorum. You ever read comics when you were a kid, Lieutenant?"

Appelbaum shakes his head and resumes the search. He pauses at Milo's boxes. Big surprise. He circles the stack like he can't quite figure it out. Now he's running his hand over the cardboard. I prefer the cop who busts in with a battering ram and starts tearing the place apart. Someone who's not afraid of a little manual labor.

He says, "You mind?" Sarcastically.

"Go right ahead."

He rips open the top box as if trying to surprise what's inside. I watch his face for the punch line.

He's intrigued. Maybe the guy's a closet romance fan. He takes out a course packet and starts reading.

This must be one of Milo's best students. Appelbaum is hooked from the start, an intense look on his face. He strokes his mustache, wipes his forehead. After a minute or so he puts down the paper and gives me a look of disgust.

"Fucking amazing," he says. "You don't miss a trick."

His reaction seems a tad extreme. I say, "You'd be surprised what a market there is for it." I'm feeling defensive on Milo's behalf.

Now he's looking over at Putz. "What is he, fourteen?" he says to me. "Son of a bitch. Fucking unbelievable."

"That's the whole idea."

He's angry now. "I'm taking this one," he says, hefting the top box and shoving it under his arm.

He stops at his car, makes a big deal of turning around and pointing at me. "You are going down for this," he says.

Poor guy must be having a bad day. After he's gone I open the next box in the stack and lift out the top packet. Maybe lousy romance writing is against the law. I'm really not up on the criminal code.

10. Write paragraph which continues story on the theme of dentistry.

He comes toward me. I can't move anymore but I don't care, I'm dizzy with desire, strapped into the dentist's chair, aching for the hot, throbbing gristle of his . . .

I dial the phone.

"Yes?"

"This second batch of boxes, Milo? It's, uh, not the same as the first."

"Hello?"

"I've never even *heard* of a correspondence course in writing porn!"

"What? Hello?"

"I'm in a lot of trouble here."

"Hello? Hello?"

"Come on, Milo, you can hear me."

"Hello? Is anybody there?"

"I'm going to tell your wife."

"Hello? Hello?"

I hang up. Putz is over by Milo's boxes, reading.

"Put that down!"

He drops the paper. "Jeez, Jack, don't have a Holstein."

I'm losing my cool. I dial Gina and get her machine.

"Gina, it's Jack. I won't be able to make it back tonight. I'm caught up in something. You want to grab a pizza tomorrow night? In or out, you decide. With or without anchovies. On second thought let's go out. Afterwards we'll go somewhere with a view and neck. We can take my cab, there's no stick shift—"

"Hello."

"Gina!" I wait for the onslaught. Fuck you Jack, you measly little worm, you piece of shit, that sort of thing.

It doesn't come. She says, "I can't talk right now."

"What is it, you've got company?"

"The police are here."

The police. How polite of her. The guy must be standing right next to the phone. "That Lutz guy again? Asking about your picture?"

"Yes."

"Oh, shit. Did he hear my message? Did I say my name? I can't even remember."

"I think so."

"What are you going to tell him? I know, say it's long distance. Say I'm your old high school friend Reba, calling from New Jersey. We haven't seen each other in ten years. Has he asked about me?"

"I've got to go."

She hangs up.

And you keep hearing there aren't enough patrolmen on the street.

I throw a few shirts in the back of the Checker, moving fast now. Home is becoming too damn hot. "Listen, Putz, I may need you to meet me somewhere, keep me posted on things."

"What's going on, Jack?"

"Don't know yet. But it wouldn't be a bad idea for me to vacate the premises for a few days. I'll catch you later, man."

"Hey, man."

I stop. "What?"

"Here's for luck." He tosses me a black vinyl card holder. It's an official Agent of SATURN badge, available for $1.50 and three proofs of purchase from Turbo-Pops fortified breakfast cereal. It's made out of shiny aluminum plated gold, stamped with sunburst and oak-leaf cluster.

"Thanks, Putzman."

"Don't mention it. Take care."

I rev the Checker up the slope as the garage door closes behind me. Think I'll catch Thacker before he goes home. Time to up the ante.

It's five o'clock and most of the pier offices are already emptied out. Eddie's Cutlass isn't around. The office of Thacker Enterprises is unlocked.

Patricia's desk has been cleared off and looks like all the other empty desks. The rubber plant has been moved back to the opposite corner. The rack of time cards is empty.

Thacker's voice comes from the other room, tense and clipped.

"You'll get it," he says. "Yes. Yes, I will. Of course I will. Don't worry. I said you'll get it!"

The sound of a phone being slammed down. I open and close the outer door loudly, step into view.

Thacker sits at his desk pretending to look over a stack of invoices. He acts surprised to see me. "I thought you weren't coming back. Eddie said something about another job."

"You know Eddie, he gets things wrong. Is Patricia gone? I didn't even get to say good-bye."

He stares at my bruised jaw. "I mailed your final check this morning."

"That was a bad idea."

"You'll have it in a day or two."

"I meant letting me go. You know, you really could use me, Frank."

He leans back in his creaky chair. He looks tired. "How is that exactly?"

"Unless of course you trust Eddie not to fuck you over. Then I'm just deadwood."

"Why shouldn't I?" Trust Eddie, he means.

165

I shrug. "It's nothing solid. Just that he tried to kill me this morning. Last night, too."

Thacker turns red through the tan. Can't fake that reaction. "What?"

"Don't worry about me, I can defend myself. What's important is Eddie has got something funny going on the side. Something to do with that shipment coming in from Hong Kong on Saturday. I thought you might need somebody to keep an eye on him."

Thacker comes forward in the chair, his voice low and threatening. "Funny like what?"

"I'm not exactly sure. I could find out for you, though."

"I don't even know who you are."

"Yeah you do. I'm a guy on parole looking for a job."

He considers this for a while. Finally he says, "Let me know what you find out." Accompanied by a hard look.

I say, "Is this a time card thing?"

When I get to the Bilge, DeMarco's already there. I was hoping for time to shoot the breeze with Maury the Mariner, psych myself up for the meeting. Evidently DeMarco likes showing up early to places. Except for the previous time, when he was nearly too late.

DeMarco's sitting sideways to the bar, leaning on one elbow with a straw in his mouth. His drink is strawberry red with crushed ice. He's entitled. He's watching a Marauders game on the TV over the register.

"Jack," he says with a loose smile. He's acting a little too familiar about the place, like Sigi does at her restaurant across the freeway.

I say, "Those Marauders. Break your heart every time."

DeMarco flips the straw upward like FDR's cigarette holder. "You a betting man, Jack?"

"Now and then. Once I picked six but lost the ticket. Went through half a dozen trash cans looking for it. Ended up finding a diamond ring, which I sold for five hundred bucks."

He nods. "Let's get a table."

We sit in the corner near the foosball machine. Maury the Mariner comes over and slaps down a beer without my saying a word. DeMarco looks impressed. Score one for me.

I say, "How'd you find me in the first place, anyway?"

DeMarco grins. "Guess."

"Bailey kept notes."

He shakes his head. "Saw you go into Morgenstern's that first time and ran your plates. Found out about your record and figured you were worth following around."

"Badly."

He acts hurt. "I don't get a lot of practice tailing people."

"On-the-job training is the best kind," I say, and rap my glass against his.

"So Jack," he says. "You ready to play?"

I like his choice of words. "I just came from Thacker's," I say. "He wants me to keep a close eye on Eddie."

"How'd you manage that?"

"Those two didn't trust each other from the start. Hated each other, in fact. That's our in."

DeMarco squints and says, "How can you tell?"

"Just the way they are together. Thacker's from the street, just like Eddie, you can hear it in his voice only he tries hard to hide it. Eddie thinks Thacker's a phony, puts on airs. Thacker's scared of Eddie so he acts real tough. But it's tricky acting tough in Top-Siders."

DeMarco nods at this profound wisdom. "So you play on that."

"Pretty much. The trick now is getting that container away from the both of them. Then use the box to get Eddie to a special place."

"Special?"

"Where we nail him for killing Bailey."

"How are we going to do that?"

"He doesn't like me much. Probably looking all over town for me right now. I figured we'd use me as bait. Get him to confess with you listening in."

"And Thacker?"

"We'll use the same container, right afterwards. Cops haul Eddie off first, then I call up Thacker."

DeMarco stirs his drink. He hasn't drunk much, but neither have I. He's putting it all together in his head. "It could work," he says.

"Unless you have a better plan." Which is a bluff. If I'm going to play with DeMarco, it has to be my ball.

"I was sort of thinking along the same lines," DeMarco says.

"I had a feeling," I tell him.

Twenty-five

THE DOOR DOESN'T OPEN EASILY, I have to kick it in. Part of the frame collapses in a cloud of dust and something small and black scurries away. I've always wanted to do that.

The door is the back entrance into the abandoned office building where Agent Bailey was killed. Out front police tape is strung across the entrance like a tamper-proof seal on a bottle of aspirin. Either the cops don't know about the other way, or they don't care.

From the stairs comes the flutter of pigeon wings. They get in through holes in the skylight. Now they're walking around like they own the place, which they do. Sunlight shines down in a dusty beam on the spot where Agent Bailey hung from the block and tackle. On the floor beneath it is a big dark stain.

Things have been tossed around. Bailey's makeshift desk lies in pieces. Here and there I can make out the residue of fingerprint powder. Shit, I hate this place.

I reassemble the desk, find an empty barrel for a chair. The other chair was the crate that I tore to bits, so there's no accommodation for guests.

From the window there's an excellent view of the ware-house across the street. I wonder what Bailey did to pass the time, if he just sat here and stared out. Dreamed of being a Customs inspector, I guess. Not the way I would go, but every man has to find himself.

This is my office now. Funny to think I've never had one before, not unless you count the Checker. Name on the door in gold letters, very own IN basket, gold and leather pencil cup, picture of my sailboat on the wall . . . wouldn't be half bad. Melanie Robinson must be getting to my brain.

A pigeon lands on the desk and clucks at me. I shoo him away. Within minutes I'm bored stiff. Just before leaving I adjust the window so it's a couple inches wider than before. Just a little something to get Eddie Fell's attention.

It ain't no executive suite, but it'll have to do.

This park in the Heights, it has a tremendous view of the southern half of the city, stretching from bay to ocean and miles down the peninsula. The catch is you have to climb about a hundred steps to get there. The park's on a hill and built like a Mayan pyramid, alternating steps with terrace in five tiers. By the time I reach the top I'm flat out of breath. You don't build stamina driving a cab.

Sigi's sitting on a bench at the top with her legs crossed, enjoying the view. She's wearing a loose off-white pantsuit with a cream-colored silk blouse, and big brown duotint sunglasses. The wind lifts her hair. Putz relayed her call.

I say, "You look like an angel up here."

She snorts. "I didn't come here for a picnic."

Tennis balls are popping in the distance. "It's too nice a day to be indoors. How's Ingmar?"

"There was a staff meeting this morning. The office closes at the end of the month."

"I'm sorry about that."

"Ingmar is putting his mother in a home."

"That can be all right. I hear there are some nice ones."

"Thirty-five years in the business," she says bitterly. "Thirty-five years and then . . ." She opens her hand like a magician releasing an invisible dove.

The view is hazy today. The mountains to the south are smudged lines on the horizon. Sigi puts her purse on her lap.

"So Sigi, you called."

She takes a deep breath. "I looked in Ingmar's private files. The ones he keeps in his trophy case. The sailings on that list . . ."

"Go on."

"What they had in common was, in each case they pulled back a container."

"Which they originally took to the terminal with a bunch of other containers, then a few hours later they pulled the one back. Before it ever got loaded on the ship. And always by Rollaway Trucking."

She looks at me in astonishment. "You *knew* this?"

"Well, I pieced it together."

"Then what am I doing here?"

"Helping. Go on about the shipment due in tomorrow."

Sigi hesitates. "Why don't you just arrest Ingmar now? Why don't you just arrest *me*?"

"Nobody's arresting Ingmar. That's what I've been telling you. Now go on."

"I don't know much more. Only that the container, the one that's coming in tomorrow, it's the same one we lost. Evidently Rollaway didn't pick it up in time."

Eddie Fell screws up. Maybe on purpose. "We're talking about the container that went to Hong Kong."

"Right," she says.

"Full of Buddhas."

She shrugs. "I suppose."

"And maybe coming back with a little something else."

She stands up. "I'm leaving."

"No, wait."

"It's you who should be telling me!"

"I need you, Sigi. I need a favor."

She looks at her watch, sits back down. She shakes out her hair in a way that seems kind of vain. I wonder if she likes me. One thing I've learned about women, you can't take open hostility at face value.

She says, "Well?"

I feel another brainstorm coming on. "I need a container."

"A what?"

"Twenty feet long, and green, just like the kind Thacker uses. And empty. On a chassis. Just to borrow for a couple of nights."

"May I ask what for?"

"It has to do with nailing Thacker. Beyond that I'm not authorized to say."

"And what about Ingmar? What should I say to him now?"

"Don't say anything. Not for a couple of days at least."

"You promised, Jack."

"Don't worry, I'll keep it. Ingmar is completely safe. At worst he might have to testify."

She sits up with a start. "That is not what you promised! This Thacker, he murders someone, and you want Ingmar to *testify* against him? Are you crazy, Jack?"

"I don't mean they'd put him on the stand or anything. We're talking about behind-the-scenes cooperation. But it probably won't even come to that. Chances are they'd leave Ingmar totally alone. I mean, the guy's a legitimate businessman, thirty-five years in. They take that sort of thing into account."

Sigi purses her lips. I wish I could see her eyes. She says, "What if I tell him and make him swear?"

"Not to tell Thacker? Unh-unh, not good enough. Look,

all I need is a couple of days and a green container. When it's over Ingmar will be a hero. Probably keep the office open for another thirty-five years. And make you a partner out of sheer gratitude."

"I am not doing this to become a *partner*." Indignant. But I've got her.

"I didn't mean to suggest you were. All you want is what's best for Ingmar." Joe Empathy. Why she cares so much, though, I can't guess.

"When would you need this container?"

"Tomorrow, noon at the latest. I need time to set up."

Sigi shoulders her purse and stalks off. I watch her take the steps in heels. I'll never know how women do it.

But I like the sway of her back.

"A warehouse, Jack?"

"Nothing fancy. Just a place in the city I can use for a few hours. Don't worry, it's all legal."

Freddy Fubar's on deadline. *GIGO* hits the stands in forty-eight hours and he doesn't have time to talk. Three or four kids in leather are tapping away at the computers, their skateboards leaning against the wall. Two phones are ringing in the background. Otherwise it's dead quiet. The place feels like an insurance office.

"I share space in a warehouse, Jack. Can't afford a whole one."

That's where he keeps the bootlegs, along with back issues of *GIGO*. "Whatever," I say. "Only I've got to be able to back a container into it. Like I said, it's just for a few hours. After that I'll be gone like the wind."

"Can you get your hands on any more of that cheap vinyl? I'm running out."

"I can get you some. Give me ten days."

Fubar curls his lip. It's the Elvis curl but he doesn't know it. He scribbles an address on a notepad. "There ought to be some keys around here somewhere. Try the utility drawer in the kitchen."

"I owe you, Freddy."

"Plus you'll help pass out the paper?"

"Right."

A kid who can't be more than fifteen with a negative Mohawk dumps a stack of CDs on the desk. Fubar flips through them and hands me a couple, My First Booger and Suddenly, Last Supper.

"Gee, thanks, Fred."

"They're boots. You want to do a couple of reviews, I won't complain." Ask a favor from Freddy, you pay for it.

"No prob. I expect to have some free time in a few days."

But Fubar's already on another wavelength. He's showing a kid with shoulder studs how to use PageMaker.

I'm in the kitchen when he calls after me. "By the way," he says, "Michael never turned up, but his shit did."

My predecessor at Thacker Enterprises, the one who quit so suddenly. "Where?"

"They ended up in a crawl space at the Benna Street squat. Now Jen has them. What's left of them."

"Jen?"

"Ruben, Rubenstein? His girlfriend, or was. Saw her over the weekend. Skinny kid with spiked hair. Talked about hitching a ride home to Seattle, she's probably gone by now."

"Call me if she shows up, okay?"

"Yeah, sure." But he's already back at the computer. The Perry White of the punk set.

I go by the place on Benna Street, a three-story Victorian with boarded-up bay windows and no front steps. There's a CONDEMNED sign nailed to the front door and another one wired to the fire escape. The door beside the garage hangs off its hinges. I push it open.

What used to be the garage is full of planks and chicken wire and beer cans. The place smells like piss and mildew. An orange messenger bike with two big baskets leans against a wall. Music's coming from above.

I go up the inside stairs. The living room floor is heaped with dirty blankets and sleeping bags. There's a bong in one corner, cigarette papers in another, and some old issues of *Thrasher*. Putz's favorite.

Another flight of stairs. I climb to a landing with no railing, at the head of a dark, narrow hallway. Several layers of flowery wallpaper are peeling away. I tear some off and it crumbles in my hand. Like peeling a scab.

The music is coming from the end of the hall. I pass open doors on both sides with rooms full of garbage. I know now why they call it a squat. No way you can lie down in one of these places.

I step over a hole in the floor and push open the last door. The music hits me like a gust of wind. I can't place the band but it's loud and metal, coming from a boom box lying on the floor with its speakers up. It isn't bad. Next to the boom box is a mattress with a girl or woman on it. I can't tell because she's lying face down. She has on a silk paisley vest over a white T-shirt, and blue jeans with a hole in the crotch. Her feet are bare and dirty. She must weigh eighty pounds.

I nudge her shoulder. No response. I shake a little harder and she stirs. On my third try she groans and pushes me away. I turn her over.

She's sixteen, maybe seventeen. Her face is dead pale, her hair long and stringy. She's wearing poorly applied eye makeup and her eyes are unfocused. Freddy Fubar hates this kind of thing. He won't let drugs in the house.

"Jen Rubenstein?"

I have to shout to be heard. Her mouth moves but nothing comes out. I switch off the boom box. The tape holder beside it says DEMO.

I say, "What did you say?"

She's still mumbling. "Ruben? Stein?"

"That's you, right?"

She shakes her head. "Jen's gone."

"Know where she went?"

She looks directly at me. "Do I look like I know anything?"

I'm about to turn the music back on when there's a crashing sound downstairs. I sprint down the hall to the living room and look out through cracks in the boards. Down below are two cop cars, flanking the Checker. The door to the cab is open and a uniformed officer is peering inside with a flashlight. Now I hear multiple voices and radio squawk from close by. They're in the living room and headed my way.

Back down the hall to the room with the wasted girl. I kick open the back door leading to the yard. No stairs on this side, either. I dangle off the landing and drop fifteen feet to the ground. Luckily I land on sand. But it's hell on the knees.

I scale a high fence just as a cop appears in the upstairs doorway. He yells something but I don't stop for clarification.

Twenty-six

■■
■■

"PSST! GINA!"

I'm hiding behind a scenery flat at the studio that Gina shares with a theater group and a couple of other artsy types. It's in the basement of a ten-story remodeled office building near Civic Center. They stick the culture underground. I've cut through a side entrance which passes through the Tex-Mex barbeque joint at street level, then down the back stairs.

"Fuck, Jack!"

The kid Gina's shooting is startled. Luckily his mother has gone to the bathroom. He's ten years old and wearing a cowboy outfit with chaps. He's already done seven commercials, one with national distribution. You probably know him as the little brat whose face falls into the plate of spaghetti sauce. The price of fame.

Gina tells the kid to take a break for grub. She joins me behind the flat.

She says, "Do me a favor, will you? Just wait here one sec while I call the police."

I can tell she's bluffing. But she's genuinely pissed that I lied to her. "Gina, what is going on?"

"Fucking cops took me down to the station and interrogated me for two hours. Christ, it was a fucking nightmare. They kept asking if I was Bailey's girlfriend, can you believe it? I almost said I was, just so I wouldn't have to admit I was hanging around with the likes of you."

"But you did say my name."

"No, I didn't. They did. Asked me how long I've known you, that kind of thing. What you do for a living. What *have* you been doing for a living, Jack?"

Shit, I think, maybe the cops have my wallet after all. Been toying with me all along. I say, "I can't understand how they found me."

"Apparently somebody saw you on the street with Bailey. They wouldn't say who."

"So what do they think, I killed him?"

"It's a logical assumption, wouldn't you say?"

"But you don't think that, right?"

She turns away and mutters an answer. "No."

I grab her by the arms and turn her back around. "Gina. This is important. What exactly did the cops say about me?"

She thinks for a moment. "It seems you and Bailey were involved in some kind of dope deal. That part I don't believe either."

"Thank you very much."

"Don't get cocky. Anyway, you had a falling-out, he hit you with a big stick, you managed to chain him up or something, then you stuck him on a meat hook"—she shudders, it's only natural—"and took off. That's the picture I get." She stares at me. "I remember you hurt your head right around then. You said the garage door fell on you."

"Did I say that?"

She twists away from me.

"Gina, wait. It wasn't like that." I tell her about finding

the Buddhas, getting busted by Agent Bailey, even the hand-cuffs. I show her the marks on my wrists.

"You still have the handcuffs?"

"I threw them off the bridge."

"Brilliant move."

"I can't anticipate everything."

A throat clears. I peek around the scenery flat and there's Putz, holding a couple of paper bags.

"Heya, Jack."

"Putzman!" We exchange high fives. "Glad you could show."

Gina comes out. "What the hell is this?"

Putz blushes, his cockiness melting away. "Hi, Gina."

"Jaaack—"

"It's all right, Gina, I asked him to come."

"He's a minor and you are a fucking fugitive!"

"Calm down. Hold on a sec. Whatcha got there, Putz?"

He holds out the bags. "Some shirts and socks in this one, plus a few comic books, also that picture frame you wanted, and a burger and salad from the San Antonio Grill in the other. I had 'em leave off the onions like you said."

I grab the bag with the food. I'm so hungry the smell makes me feel faint.

"Great," Gina says. "Now he's your servant."

Putz says, "Jack, I've gotta talk to you."

I silently ask Gina for some privacy. She stomps into her office across the hall and slams the door. "Okay," I say, "shoot."

"It's my dad, I think he knows."

"About the tray?"

"Yeah. Somebody's been searching around in my room. And my dad talked to that cop for a long time. I think I'm in deep shit, Jack."

"Chill out, man. Stay loose. It'll work out."

"I don't know. I'm nervous as hell. Can I hang with you for a couple days?"

"Not a good idea. But hold on a minute. Stay here, I'll be right back."

I leave him by the scenery flat and go into Gina's office. She's bent over her desk, looking at proof sheets through a loupe. Pretending I don't exist.

I say, "You know that back room with the cot?"

"Dream on," she says without looking up. "How'd you get in here, anyway?"

"How 'bout I leave off some of my clothes and a tooth-brush? Seeing as how there aren't any at your place."

Little dig there. I can't help it.

"Jack, the day one of your *shoelaces* shows up under my bed is the day I move out. Anyway, I can't be mixed up in this."

"Whole thing'll be cleared up in a matter of days, a week tops. I swear it. So it's okay for Putz to spend the night here?"

"You've got to be kidding."

"Just till his dad cools off. He's a good kid, he can help you in the darkroom."

Gina sighs.

"Thanks, babe. You're the best."

I lean over and kiss her. She meets me halfway.

"I'll try to call," I say.

"Don't bother," she says.

I don't take Gina too seriously. She'll cool down eventually. She needs her space.

I'm severely hobbled, however, by the loss of the Checker. It took me fifty minutes to get from Benna Street to the studio by bus. Now it's late afternoon and I'm review-ing my options. Home and Gina's are out, for obvious reasons. The cops may already know about Milo. The Bilge is too big a risk. And forget about the hotels. Chances are my picture's on the front page of the afternoon paper on every street corner and hotel lobby in town. CABBIE SUSPECT SOUGHT IN DRUG SLAYING. I just hope they didn't use one of Gina's nudes.

It's two buses and another fifty minutes to Thacker's office on the pier. It takes fifty minutes to get anywhere in this town by bus, never mind the time of day. On the way over I think about how to approach him. He may even like the idea that I'm a criminal on the lam. Either that or he'll call the cops himself. But that I doubt. What he needs is to lie low until tomorrow, when the container comes in.

Turns out I've underestimated his capacity for lying low. Thacker is gone. Not the furniture, which was leased. Desks, chairs, typewriter, hyphenation dictionaries, even the rubber plant—all still there. The sign on the door still says THACKER ENTERPRISES. Only the safe and the picture of the sailboat are missing, which means he is, too.

I stop a man on the mezzanine who's about to go into his office two doors down. He's wearing a Hawaiian shirt and white pants. His door says HUKILAU TOURS.

"The guy who had that office," I say. "When did he move out?"

The man frowns. "No more'n two hours ago, if that. They made one hell of a racket."

Three-hundred-pound safe and all. The bastard must already be on his pleasure boat. I'm thinking about where he might keep it tied up so I don't notice who's following me along the mezzanine. Not until he sticks something sharp in my back.

"Just shut up and come along," says Eddie Fell.

I do as I'm told. There in a red zone sits the familiar red Cutlass, death trap with eight cylinders. Eddie has a finger in my belt loop. He slips the weapon in his leather jacket, opens the Cutlass on the passenger side and pushes me in. No choice this time.

I say, "Looks like Thacker lost his lease."

For a change, Eddie's in the mood for conversation. He says, "Shut up and listen to me. I already know he's gone and I also know the cops are after your ass. But he was my partner and now I need somebody to help pull this off. You'll be on watch down at the warehouse when I pick up that container. You see anything suspicious—cops, Thacker, *anything*—you call me on the cell phone. Then I go to a second place. That's where we meet our connection and split the cash. I get seventy-five percent. You don't like it, eat shit. Twenty-five percent'll be more money than you've ever seen in your life. Okay with you?"

"You didn't need Thacker before."

"You don't know jackshit. You in or not?"

"Want to tell me what's in the box?"

"Nope."

"What if you don't show up?"

"I'll show up. And you'd better too."

"You giving me a choice here, Eddie?"

"Yeah, you got a choice."

We've been driving away from the waterfront toward the warehouse district. Now we're stopped in the middle of a gravel road with a scrap metal yard on one side and a polluted creek with houseboats on the other. The houseboats look like the town where Popeye lives. There aren't any people in sight. I can feel the V-8 engine rumbling beneath me. Eddie looks straight ahead, both hands on the wheel, dead still.

I say, "What time you want me to be there?"

Twenty-seven

EDDIE DROPS ME IN THE MIDDLE of nowhere. I spend the night in a watchman's shack at an auto impound yard that's been shut down for seismic work. I know about it because the Checker's been towed there twice. The shack has a semi-comfortable easy chair and is reasonably sheltered from the elements. Not so bad when you clear away the cobwebs.

Next morning I'm stiff, dirty and hungry. I wake to find a big brown rat staring at me from eighteen inches away. The place is thick with dust and so am I. I'm beginning to blend in with my surroundings.

I stumble into the dawn of a gorgeous day. The sky ranges from deep pink to deep blue and there isn't a cloud in it. The air feels prickly from an inland wind. It's going to be a day of electric shocks.

The one advantage to my appearance is it makes me look less like me. I follow the smell of bacon to a waterfront diner which isn't much bigger than the watchman's shack. The waitress there doesn't like me so I put my money on the counter. A five and two ones, to be exact, and forty-seven cents in change. It's enough for a plate of scrambled eggs and sausage, coffee and juice. The food tastes great.

Outside the diner there's a newsrack. I buy a morning paper and find the story on page one, picture and all. Wouldn't you know it, it's my mug shot. I was in a bad mood that day so I look dangerous. I sit on the wooden railing overlooking the bay and read the story. It's mostly what Gina said, me and Bailey in a falling out over a drug deal. The stuff on me I couldn't care less about, it's what they're doing to Agent Bailey that ticks me off. Pure libel. But the man is dead and can't defend himself.

There are witnesses who saw the two of us go into the warehouse, and me come out. Smart of the killer to use the back door. Also the UPS delivery man who blocked my cab when Bailey arrested me. Worst of all, they've got hair and blood samples from the plank that was used to clobber me. And I'm sure there's more, the cops always hold something back.

The tide is out and seagulls are picking over a stack of old tires. I've taken care of the food thing but I need to get cleaned up. The Press Club wouldn't let me in the door. I kill the two hours with a newspaper that can be read in twenty minutes. I read the bad comics, the society page, the stock tables, even the classifieds. Somebody's looking for one of those ratty little terriers that's better off lost. There's an opportunity to earn five hundred dollars a week while working at home. Bunky wants to hear from Pumpkin Breath ASAP. I wonder if I pretended to be Pumpkin Breath whether Bunky would let me use her shower.

Nine o'clock, and I go to a phone. I ask for Agent DeMarco and the receptionist tells me to wait. I have a strong feeling he gets to work on time. While I'm waiting a cop car pulls up to the diner and the cops go inside. Finally DeMarco comes on the line.

"DeMarco."

"Squire."

A pause. "Where are you?"

"You ready for today?"

"I think it's better that you come in." That Jack Webb monotone is back. No trace of the guy who likes strawberry drinks.

"You know I didn't kill him, Paul."

"You run, you look guilty."

"So I turn myself in. Then what? How are we going to get Fell and Thacker if I'm rotting in jail? Think about it, Paul."

Another pause. I wondering if he's signaling somebody to tap the line. "I'd be aiding and abetting."

"For a good cause."

"I could lose my badge."

"You know Thacker cleared out of his office yesterday?"

"Didn't hear that."

"By the way, I talked to Eddie. I mean he talked to me."

"About what?"

"I'm in a phone booth near Rosie's Café, Pier 52. I'm getting restless, Paul."

One last pause. For a second I think he's hung up. "Give me fifteen minutes."

It takes him ten. The green Rabbit parks at the café next to the cop car. I'm still sitting on the railing behind the phone booth, throwing bits of gravel at the pigeons. They're not fooled. DeMarco comes up behind me.

He says, "Pretty public place."

"It's okay. I'm disguised as a penniless bum."

I feel even dirtier next to DeMarco, who's wearing aviator shades, dark blue FBI suit with red striped tie, and loafers with tassels.

I say, "You just get a haircut?"

"What did Fell say?"

This isn't DeMarco's day for small talk. "Basically, either I agree to make a shitload of money or die."

"Doing what?"

"Being at the receiving end of today's delivery. In case

anything goes wrong. Then we split seventy-five/twenty-five. Guess which share is mine."

"He say what's in the container?"

"It's his little secret."

"He's lying to you."

"Really? You think so, Paul?"

"No way he'll show."

"That's okay, neither will I."

"What's your plan?"

"Okay. Eddie arrives at the pier for his container. Everything's in perfect order. He hooks up and starts out of the yard. At the last minute, a Customs inspector stops him."

"Me."

"You. 'Excuse me, sir, could you come into the office for a moment, please?' Eddie, of course, is scared shitless. But he's tough so he decides to play it out. In fact it's nothing, just a stupid question about paperwork. He gets out of the truck and goes inside. Which is when I climb in and drive the truck away."

"You steal the truck."

"It's hardly stealing. He's been cleared, got the papers and everything. Call it a change of drivers."

"Then what happens?"

"I take the container to another warehouse. Then I call Eddie on his cellular phone. I say, 'Eddie, it's Jack. I have your container. Let's talk.' "

"At which point Eddie comes over and breaks you in two."

"Well, there's that. Only I have something he wants. First thing he'll want to know is, where's the container? The price will be his confessing to the murder of Agent Bailey. And there you'll be, hiding with a tape recorder. After that I take him to his container and you make the arrest. And boom: We've got him for murder plus whatever's in the box."

"Where are you proposing to hold this meeting?"

"Same place where Bailey was killed. Poetic justice. Also it's convenient."

"And where's the container going to be?"

"Thacker's warehouse, right across the street."

DeMarco shakes his head. "Too complicated. I say we arrest him at the pier, turn him over to the police."

"Then he'll never confess to doing Bailey. And the world will go on thinking Bailey was a sleazeball dope dealer, and that I killed him. Plus which, you get him at the pier, he'll just deny knowing what's in the container. It's a simple plan, Paul. No way it can go wrong."

DeMarco watches a ferryboat full of commuters approaching the dock. The cops come out of the diner.

DeMarco says, "My boss would never allow it."

"That's why I'm an independent contractor. Bosses get in the way of personal initiative."

He looks at me. I can see my reflection in his glasses. I look like shit. "After this," he says, "you go to the police. Or I'll take you there personally."

The black-and-white is backing out of the lot. "After this," I say, "the police aren't going to want anything to do with me. But yeah, if you say so."

"I say so."

I wonder if he cheats on his taxes.

"Jer-ree!"

He slams the door in my face.

I knock again. "Come on, Jer, open up. I walked all the way here, took me fifty minutes."

Muffled voice. "What do you want?"

"Tell you the truth, I need a shower. Plus maybe a shave, providing you've got an extra razor."

He opens the door.

"Also I need to borrow your truck."

He slams it again.

187

"Hey, Jer? You know from bad raps, don't you?"

Half a minute passes and the door opens. Jerry's face peers out from behind it. "You kill anyone, Jack?"

"What do you think?"

He lets me in. He says, "Melanie the other day? She asked if I've seen you again."

"And you said?"

"Whattaya, think I'm crazy? But I feel like shit about lying. So I ask if it's okay to move. I'm thinking about going out to the Valley, hauling lettuce and stuff. She says she'll think about it. It'll keep me away from bad influences, she says."

I agree with him and he lets me use his shower. I pass on the shave. Twenty minutes later I look presentable again.

Jerry says, "Hey, that's my shirt."

It's the one with the dice and the showgirls and the words *Las Vegas* all over it in neon. You wear it with the tail out. "I'll bring it back with the truck. And by the way, Jer."

"What?"

"Could you lend me twenty bucks?"

It feels good to be behind the wheel again. I was not born to take the bus. I hop on the freeway and wind it out to sixty-five. I'm finally getting the hang of the gears.

Ingmar rents warehouse space on Commerce Street, about a mile south of the city, in an industrial park that's done up with landscaping and paved parking spaces and bright orange doors on the loading docks. Parked off to the side is the empty green container. Good old Sigi. The container is identical to Thacker's except in slightly little better shape. In a dark warehouse, nobody will be able to tell the difference.

I haul the empty box up to Thacker's warehouse across from my brand-new office, Agent Bailey's old lookout. Nobody stops me or gives a damn. Across the street the police tape is blowing in the breeze like a party streamer. The front door is no longer officially sealed, which doesn't matter, because there's another way in.

By the time I've backed the container and chassis into the warehouse, it's twenty minutes to the time Eddie's due at the pier. I park Jerry's truck down the street, catch a cab over to Rollaway Trucking, and ask the driver to wait around the corner.

Eddie is just coming out of the office. "You wait here," he says, as if we hadn't already gone through it all. "Keep your eyes open. Any trouble, go to 55 Anchorage Street, near Twentieth. Be there when I call."

He starts chatting with one of his fleet managers. Less than ten minutes before pickup time, but he doesn't seem to be in any hurry. He and the manager are looking over a bunch of papers in a clipboard. Then a call comes in for Eddie, and he takes it. I wonder if the cabbie has made off with my twenty-dollar bill. All I can do is sit it out.

Finally Eddie hangs up. On the way out to his truck he stops and looks at my shirt. "That's a hell of a note," he says. Then he gets in and drives off. I dash around the corner to the cab. Within two blocks we've nearly caught up with the truck. I tell the driver to stay well back of it.

"I'm telling you," he says. "Things're so dead at the wharf, I went cruising for fares down here. Airport? Forget about it. Lines're two hours long, then you get some little old lady with seven big bags who lives a mile away on the fourth floor with no elevator and don't tip worth shit. Almost gave up on the day when I saw you. Folks down here usually got their own means of transportation. I'm going home after this, crack open a beer and sit by the pool."

"Pool, huh? Not bad."

"Eah, it's an apartment pool. Ain't even heated."

"Driving a cab just doesn't pay."

"You said it, brother."

"You ought to consider moonlighting. Don't get too close to this guy, okay?"

I tell the cabbie to pull over just outside the terminal gate. I pay him off and get a receipt, tax purposes. I wait across the street behind a U-Haul truck.

Eddie lines up at the gatehouse behind fifteen other trucks. It takes him half an hour to check in at the gatehouse and drive on through. He should have shown up on time. The ship is in berth, cranes lifting one box after another like giant dipping birds. Eddie's truck disappears behind a stack of containers. I wait.

And keep on waiting. Fifteen minutes go by, then thirty. Still no Eddie. I look over to where the Customs offices must be but I don't see DeMarco, either. I check the phone on my belt. It's working.

Finally Eddie's truck appears. He's not hauling anything. This is not the plan. He pulls up and goes into the Customs building. It's another quarter of an hour before he comes out, holding his phone.

My phone rings. I push up the antenna and turn it on. "Hello?"

Eddie says, "Where the fuck are you?"

"At the second place. Saw some cops around. You got the container?"

"I fucking well do not have the container and you know it. Now tell me where it is, you piece of shit, or I'll kill you."

Twenty-eight

■■

"EDDIE I SWEAR, I DON'T know where it is."

"You stay right where you are, asshole. I'm coming over."

I watch him get into the truck and tear off in a cloud of diesel fumes. He almost takes out the edge of the perimeter fence.

Things are not working out as planned. Either the container never showed up, or somebody beat us to it. I cross over to the terminal. This time the guard in the gatehouse stops me.

"Restricted area," he says.

"That's okay. I'm here to see Agent DeMarco, U.S. Customs."

"Name?"

"Bailey."

The guard tells me to wait and picks up the phone. I figure he's been bonded. He talks for a minute, hangs up and slides open the window.

"Sorry, he's in a meeting."

"Meeting? Customs inspectors have *meetings*?"

"He can't see you right now. You'll have to call the customs house for an appointment."

It's a fifty-minute walk back to Jerry's truck. On the way I use Eddie's cellular phone to call the Customs station down at the pier. I put on my official voice and ask for Agent DeMarco. He's unavailable. He's in a meeting.

I may not have the container, but I still have a set of wheels. Now all I need is food, clothing and shelter. I've got eleven dollars and fifteen cents and an automated teller card I don't dare use. I feel like a member of Freddy Fubar's Youth Brigade, looking for a crash pad. So I drive over there. Takes me forty-five minutes to find a parking place in Freddy's neighborhood. This town wasn't built for big rigs.

A blond woman with spiked hair pushes past me at the front door and clobbers me in the knee with a giant suitcase. I limp into the computer room where the latest ish of *GIGO* has been put to bed. The screen savers are going full blast. A bunch of epidermically challenged youth are sitting around drinking beer and listening to Piss on This at maximum volume.

One of them says, "Hey, bro. Cool shirt."

I wonder what Jerry would take for it. I'm about to ask for Fubar when he comes out of the kitchen, sucking on a bottle of Calistoga water.

"Jack. You hook up with Jen? She just left here."

"When?"

"Seconds ago. You could still catch her. Just took off for Seattle."

I run outside. At first I see nothing. Then a beat-up light brown Mazda 626 driven by the blond woman with the big suitcase pulls out of a tight parking space near the corner and drives off. There's a raccoon tail on her aerial. I go after her on foot.

I almost catch her at the stop sign but she runs it. She goes left at the next corner and disappears. My knees are killing me. I tear back to Jerry's truck, two blocks back the other way, and fire up the big diesel engine. By the time I'm underway, she's gone.

I pick her up again at the bottom of the hill on the main street feeding the freeway. She's half a mile away, raccoon tail flying in the wind, lights in her favor. I cut off a guy in a black Porsche to gain ground, gun the truck to forty in a twenty-five zone. I run the red, clean miss, no contact. Now she's stopped too, and I've cut the distance in half, running up on the next pack of cars and the Mazda way out in front. The light turns green and she breaks for the on-ramp, one light to go.

The black Porsche cuts in front of me and the driver gives me the finger. He slows to a crawl. I blast the air horn, swerve right and nearly total a Honda Civic. The driver of the Civic hits the horn and slams on his brakes. I lurch ahead, weave back into the left lane, and gain another car length. In my rearview mirror I see the Porsche coming on. To him this is war. Meanwhile the Mazda has reached the last light before the ramp. The light turns red. The Mazda screeches to a halt, front tires over the limit line. The pack's shortening up and I make one last wild lane change which puts me three car lengths behind her.

I leap from the truck, run up to the Mazda and start banging on her window. Jen looks startled and won't roll it down. She has one pierced eyebrow.

She shifts into first with her foot on the clutch and grips the steering wheel with both hands, ready to fly at the green. She won't even look at me.

"I'm a friend of Michael's!" I holler to be heard over the honking and through the rolled-up window. "Michael's!" I wish I knew his last name. I pantomime riding a bike, then cranking open a car window. Just then the guy from the Porsche grabs my shoulder and swings me around hard.

"Hey, asshole," he says. He's wearing Blublockers and a nylon shirtwaist jacket with epaulets and the sleeves pushed up. "Somebody ought to teach you manners."

The DON'T WALK sign is blinking for pedestrian cross-traffic. I'm trying to ignore the Porsche driver, pleading with Jen to open up. "Michael's!" I scream, thinking that if I don't get this woman to roll down her window my life will be over. Finally Jen looks at me and I mouth Michael's name. "FUBAR!" I yell for good measure as the light turns yellow.

The Porsche driver backs off, like maybe I'm better left alone. Jen cracks open her window. "Pull over," I say, trying to catch my breath. "Other side of intersection. Got to talk to you about Michael."

Jen lets out the clutch and rolls away as the light goes green. The Porsche driver mutters something and stomps off. Cars pass me on both sides. A few of them honk. The Mazda crosses the intersection and pulls to the shoulder. Its warning lights start to blink.

I park in front of her. Jen doesn't get out of the car.

She says, "Motherfucker tell you where he was?"

"That I don't know. But his stuff. Fubar says you've got his stuff."

Her mouth opens wide. "*That*'s what he wants? His fucking *stuff*? Ha!"

"Not him exactly. Me, really. Just want to take a look."

"What'd he, borrow a shirt or something and not give it back? Typical. Anyway, I gave all that shit away."

"What did you do that for?"

" 'Cause he told me not to." This women would get along well with Gina. "Alls I got left is his tapes. And those are mine."

"Can I just see? See what's left?"

Jen groans and throws open the door, whapping my knee. "Everybody leave me alone if I do this? Let me get on with my life?" She's wearing a man's red flannel shirt over black tights with stirrups and ballet shoes. She's only about seventeen. She opens the trunk, struggles with the big brown suitcase, and flips the latches. She bends over and starts rooting through a pile of clothes and shoes, belts with studs and a hair dryer.

"Here." She throws out a pile of videotapes. They're mostly store-bought: *Ben-Hur, Gunga Din, National Velvet, The Leech People*. Except for one blank tape marked *Blue Watch*.

"Can I have that one?"

She tosses me the tape. I catch it at the knees. She slams the suitcase shut, throws it in the trunk, slams that too and gets in the car.

"Thanks," I say.

"A small price to pay," she says, and lays rubber onto the freeway.

Fubar's got a VCR in his front room just off the kitchen. The music has changed to something unrecognizable but it's still loud so I have to close the sliding door. Somebody opens it again just as I'm cueing up the tape. The music comes blasting in.

"Whatcha watching?" He's older than most of Fubar's kids, around thirty, with a grass-stained baseball shirt hanging out. He's carrying a mitt with a pack of cigarettes in it.

"Don't know yet. Could you close the door?"

"Sure, man." Seconds later it opens again and two more people come in. "Cool," one of them says. "It's movie time."

"He wants you to close the door," the guy in the baseball shirt says. My sergeant at arms.

It starts with a commercial for cold cream and a news teaser. Taped off the air. Then a station ID, followed by a shot of a flashing red light, which turns out to be on top of

195

a cop car. There's hard-edged theme music, snazzy horns mixed with sirens to a rap beat, over quick cuts of cops running into buildings and black-and-whites screaming down alleyways. Finally the title: *Blue Watch*.

"Sounds like a toilet bowl cleaner," somebody says.

"Shut the fuck up," says somebody else. The door slides open a few more times. The room is filling up.

"Good evening," says the host, "and welcome to *Blue Watch*." He's one of those craggy old actors who played G-men back in the fifties. "True tales from America's police files." From there he launches into the story of an elite undercover narcotics unit preparing to bust a major-league crack dealer who operates out of a cheap motel. We hear the cops' strategy sessions. We see them strapping on weapons under their windbreakers and the camera crew following them up the stairs. The cops' faces are electronically masked. The picture's all shaky, just like a TV commercial. Then the moment of truth. The lead cop kicks the door in and yells "Freeze! Police!" as everybody pours into this cheap motel room which is all made up for the next guest and which happens to be empty. *"Bleep,"* the lead cop says. "Son of a *bleep* mother*bleep* gave us a bum tip, I knew that *bleep* was going to *bleep* us. *Bleep!*"

At which point the host comes on to say that cops don't always win, not every time, it's just one battle in an endless war, and so on. And we break for commercials.

"Can't believe they'd show that," somebody says.

"Cops're lucky they didn't show their faces," says somebody else.

I stop the tape on a commercial for a nonaspirin pain reliever and rewind.

"Hey," somebody says, "go forward, man, not back. Let's watch the rest of the show."

I play back the scene with the cop who goes *bleep*. Then

again to make sure. Only I don't really need to because I know the voice. First time I heard it was on the phone. The strong Brooklyn accent. The unmistakable voice of Eddie Fell.

Twenty-nine

"SIGI, I NEED YOUR HELP."

"No. No more." Whispering angrily into the phone. In the background I can hear the bustle of Ingmar Morgenstern & Co., Inc.

"Just a little favor, Sigi. Last little piece of the puzzle to fall in place. Come on, help me out here."

"I'm hanging up now. Ingmar is calling me. Do your own legwork."

"Please don't hang up. Just hear me out. The container that was supposed to show up today? It never came in. Either that or somebody got to it first."

"So what?"

"So Eddie Fell is about to walk on all charges. I've got to know who has the container. Can you check to see?"

Dead air. The sound of ringing phones.

I say, "What probably happened was, Thacker snuck in early and took it away. Fooled everybody."

"Ingmar is in his office. I can't just go in there and start snooping around."

"He can't be there all the time. I mean, he's liable to take a curling break or something."

Sigi talking to someone, then back on the phone. "This is a private business. Now stop calling us here." She hangs up. Stop calling *us*. Sigi the Protector. She's trying to hold this whole thing together, single-handed, only it's not working out. Eventually the cops will make that straight shot from Thacker to Morgenstern. So will Eddie. Getting humiliated on nationwide TV can do things to you.

I want to tell Jen Rubenstein that Michael was right in getting the hell out of town. Michael's the kind of guy who sees trouble and steps aside. The world needs people like him.

I try DeMarco again, at the pier and the office. He's at neither place. No time to wait.

I've got a new plan for the empty container I borrowed from Sigi. By the time I get it into Thacker's warehouse, it's late afternoon. There was also that unplanned detour to the Roseway Arms. Now I'm back in my new and semiluxurious office overlooking Thacker's warehouse across the street. I call Eddie on his cell phone.

"Yeah."

"It's me, Edward. Jack Squire."

"Motherfucker, you are dead."

"I want to apologize for taking that container."

"I know you took it, you fuck."

"Calm down, man. That Customs agent, DeMarco? He knew about the shipment. It was Thacker tipped him off. You hear from Thacker today?"

"Don't make me laugh."

"I didn't think so. He was going to stick it to you, Eddie. Turn state's evidence to save his own butt. DeMarco was just waiting for you to drive out that gate with the container."

"How'd you know that?"

"DeMarco told me. He was the little guy that beat you up the other day, remember?"

"That's a crock of shit. He didn't beat nobody up."

"I know, it was the element of surprise. Anyway, he tried roping me into the scheme, too. I played along, couldn't tell you about it, was afraid you'd scotch the whole deal. Then where would we be?"

"All this time you knew? And you didn't say nothing? Dead, you are dead."

"You tried that several times already. Anyway, listen. I got over to the pier and pulled the container about an hour before you showed up. It was a piece of cake, DeMarco wasn't even on duty yet. Now it's safe in a warehouse and the deal's still on."

"Bullshit. I can smell a setup. And this one smells like shit."

"Why would I wait six hours for a setup? If I was going along with DeMarco I'd of let them take you down at the pier. I'm telling you, he and Thacker are out there chasing their tails. But listen, Eddie, if you're not interested, just say so. I'll take my twenty-five percent, and your seventy-five too."

"You won't live three minutes trying, punk."

"The battery on this phone's giving out. Give me a decision here."

"Where is it?"

"Pier Street warehouse."

"The fuck!"

"Thacker isn't using it. Of course he could show up at any time. Finders keepers."

"Ten minutes, you meet me there."

"I'm there now."

"Then stay. 'Cause the second time I do you, you won't walk away."

I shift my barrel chair around for a view from the window and sit back with my feet up. Eddie's taking his time. A couple of cars go by but it's otherwise dead on the street. This is how Agent Bailey sat, night after night. I take out his family pictures and stand them up on the desk. Delivered by Putz, just for inspiration.

It's a good twenty-five minutes before anything happens. Finally a van pulls up two doors down from the warehouse. Three people get out and start unloading equipment from the back. Figures that the camera crew would show up first. They're Eddie's priority now.

Another van comes from the opposite direction and stops on the other side of the door. It spews out four or five men in caps with rifles and bulletproof vests. Then a third vehicle pulls right up in front. First one out is Eddie Fell. Two smaller people follow, which makes sense because most people are smaller than Eddie Fell. Everybody's dressed in dark and bulky clothes, looking plenty photogenic.

They waste no time. Eddie leads the charge to the door. The men around him start taking it down with a battering ram. They're followed right behind by a three-man camera crew. *Blue Watch* on the scene. Agent Fell's chance for redemption before a nationwide audience.

Three tries and the door's in splinters. Now there's shouting and sirens and men pouring into the warehouse from all directions. Squad cars train bright beams on the entrance. Police marksmen take aim.

Then, silence. The cops in the street are fidgeting. I can picture the scene inside, playing out on true-life video. Eddie leads his men into the dark warehouse, weapons drawn. Flashlight play about the walls and ceiling. But the only thing in there is a single green container on a chassis. The cops approach cautiously. Careful, boys, it might be booby-trapped. Eddie's the first to reach the container. There's some kind of a noise coming from inside. Eddie can't quite make it out. He pulls up on the retaining rods and the doors swing open.

The sound from within is music. Weird music, like a dozen cheap calliopes playing out of synch. Eddie shines his flashlight into the container, the video camera peering hungrily over his shoulder.

What a shot. Two hundred Psycho Mickeys are lined up in rows ten wide by twenty deep, rocking in place, playing this crazy song: "When the Saints Go Marching In." Eddie staggers away and the video crew moves in for a better angle. Now Eddie turns and makes for the door in a rage. He bursts out of the building, looks left, then right, then straight up at the office across the street where Agent Bailey had his observation post. Eddie screams at the SWAT team and they all go barreling toward the door. They burst through the flimsy police tape and trample up the stairs, Eddie bringing up the rear. He shoves his way through the crowd of cops at the top of the stairs, and now he has a view of the room with a view of the street. But whoever was there is gone.

Thirty

■■

I REACH DeMARCO THE FOLLOWING MORNING. He's at his office, nine o'clock sharp. I imagine him all clean and spiffy in his FBI-style suit. I look like shit, having spent the night in Jerry's truck underneath the freeway. It's not a sleeper cab. I'm in a phone booth next to a schoolbus storage yard.

He says, "I told you to come in." The papers are full of me today. Profile of a major-league fence, pusher, and murderer. Jack Squire, man of many talents.

"I was busy. By the way, Eddie Fell's a cop."

I can hear him breathing on the line.

"You still there, Paul?"

"I'm here."

"What happened yesterday? At the pier."

"A cop? What kind of cop?"

"A very bad one. Why didn't the container come in?"

"Container? What do you mean?"

"Snap out of it, Paul. Fell thinks I took it. Probably because I told him I did. Now he is one very unhappy camper."

"You don't have it?"

203

"Don't I wish. Think you could check the terminal records to see if it ever came in? And if it did, who picked it up?"

"How do you know he's a cop?"

The man has a one-track mind. "I saw him fuck up on prime-time television. He's probably been on the verge of getting canned. This thing with the container was supposed to patch up his reputation, is my guess."

"And Bailey?"

"That's how badly Eddie wanted it."

More dead air. DeMarco trying to recover his Jack Webb persona. "So come in. The plan is dead."

"No it's not," I say. "It's better than ever. Fell is pissed off at me. He wants to kill me so bad he can't keep down food. All I've got to do now is call him up. He's even given me the phone to do it with, although the batteries are about to go."

"Without the container?"

"There is that one small catch. Obviously it'd be better if we had it. So we need to know who hauled it away."

"Not if Fell's undercover," DeMarco says. "No way we can arrest him for smuggling anymore."

"Paul, Paul, Paul. Think about it. The guy kills an employee of the U.S. government. Kind of makes it look like he wanted the stuff for himself, doesn't it? Whether he did or not."

"With a camera crew along?"

"He won't have one this time, I guarantee it."

A low whistle. "You know what, Jack? You're cold."

"Not cold. Just practical. So find out who picked up that container, okay? I'll hold."

Bay Dray is a short-haul trucking operation south of the city, not far from the warehouse leased by Ingmar. Next door is a U-shaped motel with doors painted in pastels. On the other side is a place that makes tortilla chips. The air reeks of them.

There's a cyclone fence around a yard full of empty chassis. Over near the maintenance building are a couple of tractors painted silver and red with a crab and the company's name stencilled on the doors. The office is a tiny glassed-in building with a potted plant and a couple of seats torn out of schoolbuses. Next to this place, Rollaway Trucking looks like Yellow Freight.

The young woman behind the counter has big hoop earrings, lots of eye makeup, and hair she either spent hours on or forgot to comb when she got out of bed. I can never tell which.

She's propped a Faulkner paperback on top of a parts catalog. Beside the book is a pocket pack of Kleenex. I say, "*The Sound and the Fury* is overrated. I prefer *Absalom, Absalom!*"

She looks up. "What?"

"Some folks like his short stories the best. Ever read 'Barn Burning'?"

"Can I help you?"

"I doubt it. Unless you have any job openings."

She sighs like she gets this all the time. "There's nothing open right now. You want to, go ahead and fill out an application, though."

"Actually I'm not unemployed. But I'm about to be."

"I'm sorry to hear that." She sounds like she means it. Must be Jerry's Vegas shirt, dirty as it is.

"Seeing as how badly I screwed up. You don't go around losing containers and expect to keep your job. Not when my boss finds out."

She marks her place with a finger and closes the book. "That's not very easy to do."

"Normally I'd say that's true. But the paperwork, it just vanished into thin air. You ever have that happen to you?

205

One moment it's right in front of your face, the next it's gone? Then it's back again?"

"I guess so."

"Only this time it didn't come back. I think it's stuck floating around in some parallel universe."

"I can't see as how one tiny thing like that can lose anybody their job."

"Normally I'd say you're right. But the truth is, I'm kind of like on probation. This was like my last chance."

"I wish I could help."

"Oh, no way you can. Not unless I was able to get a peek at your records. Showing where you guys took the container."

"We were the ones took it?"

"Yesterday. Off the *Montenegro* at Pier 80. But listen, I'd better be getting back. My boss is going to want to know what's going on. And you know what? I'm just going to tell him. I'm tired of bullshitting."

"And your boss is?"

"Thacker. Frank Thacker. Thacker Enterprises over on Pier 1. The broker is Ingmar Morgenstern."

She starts thumbing through a stack of papers on a two-ring board. The right one is near the top.

She says, "You're right. We hauled that for Ingmar Morgenstern & Company. Shown here as your broker. To the Morgenstern warehouse right over here on Commerce Avenue."

"Shit, are you kidding? Right over there? Stone's throw away? I can't believe I forgot that."

"Well, we all have our days."

"Morgenstern, I just can't believe it." I slap myself. "I'm going out to buy me some bolts to keep my head on."

She laughs. "Good luck."

"So what, you're reading that book for school?"

"Yeah."

"You know they have these Cliffs Notes, boils it all down to a few pages? Gives you the gist of things."

"Thanks for the advice."

"No sweat. I figured I owed you something."

It's the same warehouse where Sigi left me the container. And it's locked with a heavy-gauge padlock. All my equipment is either in the Checker or at home. I could also do with a change of clothes and a shower. I have the strong feeling I'm not presentable.

If only I had the Checker I could pick up a few fares and generate some cash for a meal. I pull out Eddie's cell phone to call Jerry Mack. The battery's good for maybe one more call, so I use my last quarter at a public phone.

"Jerry."

"Where's my truck?"

"That's the thing, Jer. I need it for another day."

"Are you kidding? I'm out of here tonight. I'm going to Bakersfield, for Christ's sake, then L.A. Whattaya, want me to fly?"

"Cross my heart, you'll have it back tonight. There's just this one last little thing I have to do."

"You know the cops were here yesterday? Asking about you? I think they're watching me now. Three times today a car drives by the house."

"I'll leave the truck down by the gas station, I won't even knock on your door. If they catch me I will disavow any knowledge of our friendship. And I'll be back by midnight at the latest."

I hang up before he has a chance to argue. The trouble with Jerry is, he worries too much.

I drive over to Morgenstern's, park half a mile away and pass the time reading Jerry's porno magazines while jets roar overhead. Twice my cellular phone rings. I don't answer it.

From the truck I watch cars leaving the lot outside Ingmar Morgenstern & Co., Inc. I recognize Ted's motorcycle, Richard's 4x4, Ingmar's sleek black BMW. Last out is Sigi, loyal Sigi. She drives past without seeing me. There's a determined look on her face.

I give it another fifteen minutes. The sun's gone behind the hills but there's still plenty of light. I cover the distance on foot. I hope nobody changed the code. I unlock the door, rush over to switch off the alarm, and call the alarm company like before. The woman on the line is polite, even seems to recognize my voice. So much for that.

I go directly to Ingmar's office. The door is unlocked, which seems strange. I open it slowly. His trophies gleam in the twilight. The desk drawer is unlocked, too. I wonder if he's losing his edge.

There are no keys in the drawer. I look everywhere, in all of the desks in the main room, especially Sigi's, all the niches and cubbyholes I can find. Damn her. She's locked Ingmar away, nice and safe.

Back into his office. I wait twenty minutes, pick up the phone and speed-dial Sigi. Her answering machine clicks on, then she interrupts it in person, out of breath. She's just come in the door.

"Hello, wait one minute, please. Oh, damn. There." *Beep.* "Hello, who is this?"

"Your fairy godmother."

"What do you want?"

"A key, for one thing. To a warehouse over on Commerce Avenue."

Long pause. "Well," Sigi says, just to be saying something.

"Sigi, I'm getting the distinct feeling that you don't trust me."

"How did you get my number?"

"I was under the impression we had this all worked out.

You and me together. The whole point being to protect
Ingmar. Now the pieces are all in place, Sigi. It's like a chess
problem, that's how I approach it, white to mate in two
moves. I'm this close to wrapping things up, but I've got to
have that container. I mean, what good's it do you to have
it, makes you vulnerable, and Ingmar too. Whereas if I take
it away, he's safe, you're safe, and we get the son of a bitch
who killed Agent Bailey. You didn't know the guy like I did.
I've got pictures of his family. Guy with a family gets killed
like that, all you want to do is catch the bastard who did it
and make him pay. On top of which Ingmar walks, he didn't
know what was going on. Either that or they made him do
it, believe me the D.A.'ll understand. But only if you hand
over the container and trust me to play it out—"

"Okay."

"Okay what?"

"Okay I'll give you the container."

Sometimes I amaze myself. The gift of gab. "So when?"

"Right now. Meet me on Commerce Avenue in fifteen
minutes."

"Fifteen minutes, right. I'll be there. You know something, Sigi? You're beautiful. I never told you that before.
But I'm saying it now. Absolutely, positively—"

"Good-bye, Jack."

I put down the phone softly. I'm sure she likes me.

As I come out of Ingmar's office a fist slams into my
stomach.

209

Thirty-one

IT HURTS. I GROAN AND collapse into a ball. My stomach feels like it's coming up through my throat. Then a kick in the head stops me thinking about my stomach. I cover up like a pill bug while he works on my kidneys. "Motherfucker," he keeps saying. "Get up, motherfucker."

I'd rather not. But I'm a stationary target so long as I'm on the floor. I unroll and stagger to my feet as he lets loose with a right which grazes my jaw and sends me crashing into a file cabinet. My brain's telling me to stay down but my body keeps trying to get up. My body harbors a secret death wish. I'm trying to regain my balance when a woman begins to scream. She says, "Howie, no!"

Howie it is. Betty's husband hulks over me in his football shirt, wiggling his fingers for me to stand up. "Come on, shithead," he says. "Come and get some more. I'm going to take your fucking head off."

This sounds like a bad idea, but I can't seem to say it. Meanwhile Betty has thrown a body block at Howie and has her arms around his shoulders. She's like a fern clinging to a boulder.

"Howie, I told you, he's not the one!" she's saying. "Howie, please!"

Howie doesn't seem to hear. His eyes are clouded over, his nostrils are flaring, and his jaw's so loose it's about to fall off. Only now he's muttering to himself. Evidently Betty has gotten through.

She knows it, too, and loosens her hold. Howie works his shoulders like he's shrugging off a gorilla playing piggyback. "Huh," he says, as his adrenaline level drops.

Mine, too. I breathe as deeply as I deem it safe. My nose is filling with blood. "Hey," I gasp, "what gives?"

Betty says angrily, "What do you want to do, Howie, kill someone? Just tell me what you want to do."

Howie's eyes come into focus. "What?"

"I asked you a question. I said, What do you want to do? Give me a sense of things here. Would it make you feel better to beat the shit out of somebody? Anybody at all? Why not Jack? He's here already, he probably won't mind."

"Actually I would," I say, feeling for open wounds.

Betty sighs with disgust and turns away from her husband. "God," she says, "it wouldn't be so bad if I had some *enemies*."

I stagger out of the office, stopping to throw up on Howie's car. My head still hurts but the pain in my stomach is going away and there are no broken bones. Howie hits like a girl.

Even with the pummeling break I beat Sigi to the warehouse on Commerce Avenue. It's almost completely dark now. I wait in the cab of the truck and watch the stars come out, one by one. Ten minutes later her Mazda comes sailing around the corner.

Sigi has changed into blue jeans, cross-trainers and an oversized B.U.M. sweatshirt. Her hair is tied back carelessly with an elastic band. She's never looked sexier. How I look,

211

she doesn't seem to notice. "Come on," she says, leading me toward the warehouse with a handful of keys.

"Sigi, this is really great of you."

She mumbles something. Lately she's been talking to herself a lot. The keys jangle as she finds the right one and snaps open the lock.

Inside is a green container on a chassis. I stare at it for a moment. It's streaked with rust and there's a crease along one side.

"Go ahead," Sigi says, looking smug.

The big moment. I walk around to the back and open the doors. It's full of cardboard boxes, just like the others. One of them has been torn open. I hoist myself into the container and look inside.

I brush away a top layer of Styrofoam peanuts. And there, staring at me with that wicked little grin, is a rubber Buddha.

The box is full of them. That's okay, I think, there are hundreds more cartons to check. I open five more and find the same thing. Nothing but Buddhas, as far as the eye can see.

"Well?" Sigi says.

"You knew."

"Not until I looked. You want it, or what?"

Eddie's grand scheme, the priceless shipment from Hong Kong. At least he ended up with the Psycho Mickeys. Me, I've got zilch.

I grab one of the Buddhas and press its belly in frustration. Nothing comes out.

"Shit," I said. "These don't even work."

Sigi turns away and rattles her keys impatiently. Something's rattling in my brain, too. I'm thinking about that fortune I got at the Happy Assassin: WHEN THE BUDDHA IS SILENT IT IS MOST PROFOUND. I take out my pocketknife and stab the little fellow in the belly.

The knife comes out streaked with white. I rip open its belly, wedge my thumbs into the slit and pull. Inside is a torn plastic pouch full of a coarse white powder.

I squeeze a few more Buddhas. Every one of them is silent. I look at the hundreds of boxes which are crammed into the twenty-foot container, floor to ceiling, back to front.

"Oh, shit," I say.

Sigi turns around. "What was that?"

"Huh? Nothing."

"Do you want the container or not?"

Did I mention my one strict rule? No drugs or toxic waste?

"What the hell," I say with a shrug. "Might as well."

"By the way," Sigi says. "You're not a cop. You're just a sleazy guy. Now leave us alone."

And she gets into her car and speeds away.

On the way up to Freddy Fubar's warehouse, the truck runs out of gas. The gauge says it's half full. I tap the panel and the needle sinks to empty. Jerry warned me about this.

The engine lurches and sputters as I muscle the rig off the freeway. I coast the last hundred yards, coming to rest at the bottom of the off-ramp. I pick up Eddie's cell phone. It's dead, too.

I'm on a busy arterial across from a McDonald's. The play area consists of brightly colored tube slides with bubble portholes. It's full of screaming kids. I put on the flashers and lock the truck.

Cars whiz by at forty miles an hour as I try to cross the four-lane thoroughfare without the help of a stoplight. One direction clears and I dash out to the median strip. Actually it's a double yellow line about five inches wide. I look back at Jerry's truck, hooked up to the green container with the crease in the side and parked right next to a sign that says TOW-AWAY—NO STOPPING ANYTIME.

A family in a minivan tries to run me down but I make it across the street to a telephone right outside the McDonald's. A teenage girl with big hair is using it. Her cheek bulges with gum.

"And I go, 'Like wow, Christy, can you believe it?' and she goes, 'Hardly. I mean maybe in a million years,' and I go, 'He is so fine,' and she goes, 'Duh!' and I go, 'I am so stoked, I can't even believe it,' and she goes, 'Are you totally psyched?' and I go, 'Totally,' and she goes, 'I am so jealous!' Can you believe it? And I'm like dying 'cause Christy's the one been going around bragging about Tom? And she's like, 'Angela, don't be so shy,' and I'm like, 'Nothing ever happens to me, I'm just going to shrivel up and die.' I mean, my dog won't even come near me, I feel so gross. I keep looking in mirrors thinking maybe I've got this bodacious zit or something? And Christy, she can't even believe it, her mouth's hanging open like this, uuuhhhh. I mean I am cracking up, it is so funny. Here's this really cute guy—"

"Angela!"

She stops and looks me over, the uncombed hair, the bruises, the Vegas shirt, the two-day beard. "Huh?"

"Angie, is that you? Jesus, you've grown. What are you, seventeen now?"

Angela looks suspicious. "Who are you?"

"It's me, Angie! You know, Jack. My God, you have really filled out."

She says something into the phone and hangs up. "Get away from me, pervert," she says to me, and walks off in a huff, snapping her gum.

The phone is free. I get a dial tone and press O.

"Operator six-two-six."

"Yeah, Operator, listen, you've got to help me, the stupid phone ate my quarter and it's all the change I've got, I'm out of gas and I just need to make a local call."

"Number, please."

I tell her and she puts me through. Hardly ever works.

"DeMarco here."

"Listen to me, and no bullshit, Paul. I've got the right container and I'm going to put it together with Eddie Fell. You want in?"

"What's inside?"

"It ain't baby powder. Anyway listen, soon's I get some gas into this sucker I'm going to take it to a place I've got. You sit by the phone."

"Gas for what? Where are you?"

"Unh-unh. You want the stuff, the price is Eddie. We agreed."

"I can't protect you anymore, Jack."

"Won't have to. Just wait to hear from me."

I hang up before he can argue about it. Then I look around. There isn't a gas station in sight, let alone one sells diesel. But it's an industrial district, so I start walking. I pass a lumberyard, a clothing outlet, a place that sells automatic garage door openers. Three blocks down I come to a modular hut which houses an alarm company. The sign on the door says CLOSED. The yard's surrounded by chain-link fencing and there's a German shepherd asleep near the door. There's also a rolled-up garden hose, reachable through a break in the fence. Makes a perfect siphon.

I ease my hand through the crack and the dog's head pops up. I pull my hand back. The dog growls. It comes to its feet and pads over to the fence.

The hose is about eighteen inches back from the fence. The opening is narrow and jagged. The dog sits on its haunches, tongue hanging out. I hold my breath and position my hand in midair. On the count of three I thrust it through the gap. The dog hurls itself against the fence. Its fangs flash as I grab the hose and yank it back through. The sharp edge of the chain link tears into my arm. The fence rattles with the weight of the animal. My arm drips with

215

blood but I'm holding on to one end of the hose. The dog is barking like mad.

Quickly I use my pocketknife to slice off a four-foot length of the hose. From a nearby dumpster I dig out an industrial-sized stewed-tomato can, and another which used to hold paint. I even score a thin sheet of aluminum which can be rolled into a funnel. Now if I can only find a truck with a tankful of gas.

There aren't any trucks around, empty or full. I'm thinking, what the hell is an industrial area without trucks? Then I see it, just around the corner, a thrashed Mercedes sedan with a blackened rear. A sluggish, smoke-spewing diesel. Makes up for all the times I've been stuck behind those clunkers on a hill.

It has a locking gas cap. As if they were expecting somebody to come along and siphon out the gas. German car owners, they're paranoid.

The lock yields to a squiggly piece of wire which I find in the gutter three feet away. The only thing easier to open is luggage. I feed the hose into the tank and suck up a mouthful of gasoline. Yum. I have to keep sucking and spitting to keep up the flow. Every few minutes I stop to keep from passing out.

It takes me twenty minutes to fill both cans. At one point a man with thick glasses and a cap with earmuffs walks by, but doesn't say anything.

The paint can has a handle, the tomato can doesn't. Diesel fuel sloshes out as I lurch back toward the truck. When I get to the four-lane street I see a helmeted motorcycle cop in jodhpurs standing by the truck. His bike is parked to the side, near the underpass.

I wait at the curb as both directions are magically cleared of traffic. Fuck it, I think. Go for it. I stumble across the street with the heavy cans.

The cop sees me coming. "This your truck?"

"Damn thing gave out on me, Officer, no notice. Fuel gauge must be shot. Should have traded it in six months ago."

He stares at the overflowing cans. I say, "Friend of mine, down the road, lent me a couple of gallons of diesel." The cop looks dubious. "Well, you can't stop it here," he says, pointing to the sign. It's those helmets, they're way too tight. "Sorry, Officer," I say. "I'll move it right away."

The cop watches as I roll up the funnel, stick it in the tank and pour in the fuel. At last I put down the cans and start to get in the cab.

The cop says, "You just gonna leave them there?" Pointing at the cans.

"Heh-heh. Sorry." I go back, get the cans, and throw them in the truck.

Now the cop sees my bloody arm. Just then a man comes running down the street from the direction I came. He's three blocks away. The cop says, "May I see your license and registration, please?"

"Uh . . . they're in the cab, sir."

"Would you get them, please?"

The running man is a block closer, waving his arms. Looking pissed.

I climb into the cab, open the glove box and pretend to rustle around in it. "Just a minute," I say. "It's here somewhere." Meanwhile I'm slipping the key into the ignition.

The running man is just across the street, waiting for it to clear. He's shouting over the roar of traffic. The cop is getting impatient. "Here it is," I say, straightening up and with one fluid move slamming the door, locking it and twisting the ignition key. The engine coughs but doesn't respond. Nothing in the fuel line. I pump the pedal and try again. The cop starts banging on the window with his nightstick. The running man has made it halfway across the

217

street and is yelling at the cop, who finally notices him. I try the key again and the engine catches.

The cop smashes the glass of my window. I jam the stick into gear, let out the brake and start to roll. I just miss hitting the running man on my right fender. The cop leaps away as I swerve left to take out his cycle. I feel a bump underneath, yank the wheel in the other direction, and pull out into traffic. In my mirror I see the cop bent over his smashed bike and the running man gesturing wildly. Then they're out of sight.

Thirty-two

■■
■■

EDDIE FELL IS LATE. I'm sitting with my feet up on Agent Bailey's makeshift desk listening to pigeons chattering in the rafters. They seem to be multiplying. Occasionally one flutters to the floor, finds nothing, and flies back to a beam.

"He isn't coming," says the voice of Customs Inspector Paul DeMarco from behind the wall at my ear. I can just see him through the cracks.

"He'll come," I say.

"Along with half the agents in town. And a camera crew."

"I told you he'll come alone."

"What makes you so sure?"

"Because he can't afford to get burned a third time. That's part of it. Mostly because he hates me."

"Did you have to do that thing with the . . . what do you call them?"

"Psycho Mickeys," I say. "I just couldn't help myself. Not after discovering he was a cop."

"It wasn't part of the game plan."

"I like to improvise. Keeps me fresh."

"All you did was make him mad."

"Hell, Paul, I thought that was the whole idea."

Silence from behind the wall. DeMarco hates to deviate from a plan.

Five or ten minutes go by. DeMarco says, "If he confesses to the murder, I say we take him right here."

"Unh-unh. Can't have one without the other. The dope's a motive for the murder. Murder makes the dope charge stick."

Five more minutes. A pigeon lands on the desk, right between the two Buddhas. I think, Diana Ross and the Supremes. DeMarco says, "You were planning on stealing that container full of dope yourself, weren't you?"

"What?"

"You know what I mean. Only for some reason you changed your mind. Why'd you change your mind, Jack?"

"Paul. I'm hurt and offended."

A creak on the stairs. Somebody's coming in the front way. DeMarco draws back from the crack in the wall. A pause, another creak. Somebody waiting and listening. Taking his time.

The pigeon takes off into the rafters, leaving a feather behind. I lean against the window, try to look relaxed. Minutes tick by in pigeon coos and wing flaps. The far end of the room, the doorless doorway, is in near darkness. I can just make out a big, bulky figure coming slowly up the stairs. It pauses at the top, then steps into the room. Into the beam of brightness from the skylight.

"Hi, Eddie." My voice sounds strange.

I say, "You want to sit down?"

"You know what I want." A voice from someplace deep.

"Maybe you ought to sit down. Come to think of it, you can't. There was a crate here for visitors, but it kind of got wrecked."

"Cut the crap and tell me where you stashed the fucking

220

box." He's several steps closer now. He eyes the pair of Buddhas on the desk.

I pick one up and squeeze its belly. It screams. I toss it to him.

The Buddha bounces at his feet. He didn't even try to catch it.

"That one's an original," I say. "I've also got this other one here"—I pick up the second Buddha and squeeze—"doesn't make any noise. For some reason."

Eddie growls, comes closer.

I say, "Hold your horses. You don't want to kill me yet. I've still got the container."

"I say you ain't got shit."

Eddie's past the beam of light now, two steps from the desk. I'm boxed in.

I say, "I want to tell you where the container is. I really do. As far as I'm concerned, our deal's still on. With a couple of conditions."

Eddie just stands there, looking huge, pure hatred in his eyes.

I say, "First is, you won't arrest me. That goes without saying."

A vein in his neck stands out. Eddie never was much of a talker.

"Second is, on this Bailey thing, the murder. I got to say, I'm a little worried."

I think he's moved an inch closer. Hard to tell in this light.

"The fact you whacked him, that's your business. But I don't want to be the one who pays for it. So either find another scapegoat or close the case. I know you're not Homicide but you've got friends. Ways to get things done. And you can start by giving me back my wallet."

A board creaks beneath his feet.

"And just in case you're thinking about doing me here, I've got a couple of safe-deposit boxes around town."

A noise from behind the wall. Eddie doesn't seem to have heard it. He's staring at the desk. Now he sees Agent Bailey's family pictures.

Through the crack I sense DeMarco holding his breath. Eddie looks from the pictures to me. He reaches into his leather jacket and pulls out a gun. Looks like a Smith & Wesson .41 Magnum, big-bore revolver. Good for stopping charging bulls.

He points the gun at my head. "Listen to me," he says. "You got that shipment, you take me to it now. No fucking conditions. No this or that. You don't got it, you're bullshitting me again, I'll blow you away. Understood?"

My turn for silence. The Smith & Wesson is rock steady in Eddie's hand. My own hands are shaking badly. There's no sound from behind the wall. I forgot to ask DeMarco if he had a gun. The Buddha on the desk grins at me.

Eddie extends the gun another couple of inches and thumbs the hammer. Some guys just don't know how to negotiate. "Okay," I say. "You win. Let's go."

Freddy Fubar's warehouse is just under three miles away. Eddie steers the Cutlass through rush-hour traffic like a pro. The gun is back in his jacket. It's like we're running another minor errand for the boss.

Eddie has installed an outside mirror on the passenger's side. In it I can keep track of the dark green VW Rabbit following two blocks back. He already knows where we're going.

"So Eddie," I say. "What are you planning to do with your share?"

I brace for the sidewinder. Instead he drives on like I'm not even there. I notice that his knee isn't bouncing anymore. His body has gone loose and Buddha-calm. I wonder if he meditates.

So much for trying to draw him out. I'm not in the mood

for talking anyway. My own body feels like a mass of steel-wrapped cable, my stomach a block of ice. I'm wondering which is more likely: walking away with a one-quarter share of a container full of heroin imported by an undercover cop, or winning the Big Spin. I can't make up my mind.

In the mirror I see that DeMarco has closed the distance by half a block. Sloppy tailing. I wonder whether Eddie knows his car. I silently wish for him to drop back. Then I get my wish.

Eddie goes through a yellow light, which is red by the time DeMarco hits it. DeMarco runs the light anyway and broadsides a yellow Subaru. The Subaru spins clear and the Rabbit runs up onto the curb and smashes into a utility pole. The intersection turns to instant gridlock.

Eddie drives on. He doesn't seem to have noticed the smashup. Behind us people are running toward the scene from all directions as the intersection recedes in the mirror. Then it's gone.

I'm going to have to improvise.

Minutes later Eddie pulls up to Fubar's warehouse. It's a rickety wooden structure which looks like it could be toppled by a stiff gust of wind. A faded sign says HIDES AND. The warehouse is down at the end of an L-shaped cul-de-sac, flanked by the back wall of a rattan furniture distributorship and a fenced-off empty lot. There's nobody in sight.

Eddie cuts the engine but doesn't get out of the car. A minute passes, then two. Maybe he's having a change of heart. Turns out all he's doing is surveying the terrain. "This is shitty," he says, looking over his shoulder at the blind bend of the alley, and I have to agree. I had a bitch of a time backing the container into that space. Took out one of Jerry's side mirrors.

Eddie throws open the door and eases himself from the car. He seems a trifle arthritic. Could be an old bullet wound. He slams the door and ambles around to my side. Looking both ways, he draws out the Smith & Wesson and opens my door. "Out," he says.

He sticks close as I approach the warehouse and process my avenues of escape. Can't break left or right. Wouldn't make it halfway up that fence. No windows on the back of the rattan dealer. No avenues at all.

I fumble for the keys, take too long to open the padlock. Eddie grunts ominously. The padlock snaps open and falls to the ground. I bend to pick it up.

"Leave it," he says, shoving me inside.

Both of us need time to adjust to the dark. Slowly the shape of the container becomes visible. From this angle you can't see the crease in the side. In the far corner of the room is a tiny red pinprick of light. Must be part of the sprinkler system.

I reach for the light switch. "Leave it," Eddie says. He draws out a snub-nosed halogen flashlight and flicks it on. The powerful beam illuminates the back of the container, all the dents and rust spots. The only one of Frank Thacker's containers ever to make it across the ocean.

"Open it," Eddie says. I obey. The doors creak open to reveal a wall of cardboard. Eddie waves the Smith & Wesson impatiently. I climb up on the tailgate, grab a carton and let it tumble to the ground. Eddie winces.

I jump down, tear open the box. Brush away Styrofoam peanuts and pull out a Buddha. Eddie snatches it from my hand. He shoves the flashlight under his arm and produces a switchblade, *snick*. Placing the Buddha on the ground, he stabs it deep in the belly.

He guts it just like I did, sees what I saw, a plastic bag full of fine white powder. He positions the flashlight so it points at the ceiling, dabs his tongue with his index finger. He stands up.

"All right," he says, reaching behind and pulling out a set of handcuffs. "Jack Squire, you're under arrest. You have the right to remain silent . . ."

Et cetera, et cetera. I haven't got a mirror but I'm sure there's a stupid look on my face.

"Turn around," he says, shoving me against the container. A quick one-handed frisk, then the click of the cuffs. Shit, I think. Got to collect myself. Eddie swings me back around to face him. He looks cool and businesslike. No longer the raging bull.

I try to laugh. "Eddie," I say. That old Zappa song pops into my head. *Eddie, are you kidding?* "Eddie. We have got one huge misunderstanding—"

"Shut up." He takes out his cell phone and punches in a number. After a few seconds he says, "Yeah. Got one of them." He gives the address. "And the merchandise. Yeah, it's big. Get on over here but don't move in yet. Wait for my signal. Out."

He snaps the phone shut, slips it back into his pocket.

"Eddie, we need to talk. Seriously."

He's not listening. He looks at his watch and frowns. Who's he waiting for, Thacker? He jiggles the gun. Something's gone wrong.

I'm about to have another go at explaining myself when the door swings open and becomes a blinding rectangle of light. Eddie turns toward the figure in the doorway as it steps into the warehouse and becomes a shadow among the shadows. Eddie starts to say something but is interrupted by a deafening blast and his body slams against mine and we both go crashing to the floor. He's lying on top of me making strange animal noises and there's a sharp pain in my arm from landing funny. With one great bellow Eddie rolls off me, seizes up and goes limp.

225

I struggle to sit upright as the figure crosses the room toward me. He's backlit from the doorway but I can make out the shape of Customs Inspector Paul DeMarco.

Deviating from the plan.

Thirty-three

"Jesus, Paul," I say.

"You all right?"

"I think my arm's broken."

The flashlight's been knocked over and throws a beam across the floor onto the body of Eddie Fell.

"You didn't need to do that," I say. "I was handling it."

DeMarco nudges the body with his foot. Eddie's jacket and shirt are covered with blood. So is the floor beneath him. So, I realize, am I.

The pain in my arm is excruciating. "Keys to cuffs," I manage to say. "In the jacket."

DeMarco squats beside the body, dangling his gun. He digs into Eddie's pocket and comes up with a ring of keys. His knees crack as he stands up.

My arm is killing me.

DeMarco walks slowly over to the open carton and the eviscerated Buddha beside it. He picks up the mutilated Buddha and looks it over. He sticks a finger into the slit made by Eddie's knife.

"Well," he says, dropping the Buddha back into the box. "I guess that's that."

"Uh, Paul? You want to unlock the cuffs?"

He looks from me to Eddie. Hard to tell his expression in the dimness. He comes toward me with the keys in one hand, his gun in the other. Looks to be a .357 Magnum with an eight-inch barrel. Judging from what it did to Eddie.

Standing over me he pockets the keys and snaps open a white handkerchief. Eddie's dead, I'm in pain and the man is going to blow his nose. Priorities.

Instead he uses the handkerchief to remove something from the inside of his jacket, an object small and dark and square. It falls on me, bounces off my knee and comes to rest on the dirty floor.

"Thought you might want this back," he says.

It's my wallet.

"With Bailey's fingerprints," I say.

Ambush from behind, that's DeMarco's trademark. Advantage to the little guy.

Think fast.

I look around furtively. That red light in the corner off to the side, the sprinkler system. Maybe there's a way to trigger it.

Then I think, not a sprinkler system. Light's positioned too low, it should be way up near the ceiling somewhere. This one is closer to eye level.

DeMarco returns to Eddie's body and pockets the Magnum. He's looking for something, and finds it: the .41 Smith & Wesson, six feet away. He uses the same white handkerchief to pick it up.

The red light, it's a camera. A goddamn video camera. Eddie Fell filming his own bust, crewless this time. Not chancing another public humiliation.

Smile, DeMarco.

"I should have known," I say, trying my best to sound devil-may-care. "You said you ran my plates that first day at Morgenstern's but Putz says you were outside my house at seven that morning. And I didn't show at Ingmar's until eleven."

DeMarco's crouched over the body, deep in thought.

"And that's not all. On the phone Eddie threatened to 'do me' a second time. The first time was in the alley when you showed up. The other times were you."

DeMarco hefts the Smith & Wesson. He stands up and points the gun at my head.

I'm soaked in sweat. "You know, Paul, you're even stupider than I am. I mean really."

"Save it, Jack. I'm not buying."

"Come on. Haven't you figured it out yet?"

His arm stiffens and he corrects his aim. Pointing now at my heart. His scenario comes clear: Crooked cop Eddie Fell shoots vicious drug dealer Jack Squire, brave Customs Inspector Paul DeMarco bursts in and shoots Fell. Too late to save that scumball Squire.

But how did Eddie know where to set up his camera? DeMarco's the only one I told about Freddy Fubar's warehouse.

I say, "They don't give IQ tests over there at Customs?" Trying to sound nonchalant with a broken arm.

DeMarco sighs. "What's your point?"

"Let me get something out of my pocket and I'll show you."

"You've got to be kidding."

"Back pocket. Slowly. Don't put down the gun."

He nods, keeping the .41 steady. With two fingers I ease the black vinyl cardholder out of my jeans and flip it open. Showing Putz's Agent of SATURN badge. Counting on the dimness to obscure the details.

I say, "I'm a cop, asshole." I slip the holder back into my pocket as pain shoots up my arm.

DeMarco mouths the word *What?* The gun is still pointed at my heart.

I say, "Jesus, was I that good? I was sure you'd guess." Mr. Cool, with sweat dripping into his eyes.

DeMarco shakes his head slowly and smiles. "Unbelievable," he says. "Not a chance."

"You can believe it. I'm with a special division of the Justice Department. Investigating corruption in the U.S. Customs Service, Operation Rimshot. We've known from the start that you killed Ray Bailey. Just needed the proof is all."

"This is complete, absolute bullshit." But he isn't pulling the trigger. He wants to hear more. I wonder if Eddie's backup is in position yet.

I say, "Think I didn't know you were working with Fell all this time? The two of you in private communication? Christ, seems like everybody except you knew Eddie was a rogue cop. All that crap about the video crew, the TV show. The only question is, Paul, how could you blow it so badly?"

DeMarco smiles. I can almost see the lightbulb click on over his head. "Nice try," he says, almost to himself. "Real nice." He focuses in again, straightens his arm and prepares to fire.

It isn't working. He's wasted one cop already, why not another? I wonder if Eddie really called anybody on his little toy phone. Maybe he ordered a pizza.

My mouth takes off without waiting for my brain. "So make up your mind, Paul. I haven't got all day."

He smiles, first time I've seen it since the Bilge. I've managed to amuse him. "Make up my mind about what?"

" 'Bout whether you want the stuff or not. Basically this is your last chance. Eddie used that cell phone just before you took him out. So somebody'll be here any minute."

"The stuff? I've already got the stuff. I've got you, too."

"Oh, me, sure, you've got that. If that's all you want, then hell, fire away. You can frame me for the murder *and* the dope. But you won't have the dope."

"And why's that?"

"Because, bright boy, it'll be confiscated as evidence and you'll be celebrated in story and song as Customs Inspector of the Year. End up on the cover of the in-house newsletter with Rusty the Dope-Sniffing Dog. Not the same thing as the profits from a container full of heroin, is it? I mean, that *was* your original intention, wasn't it? Cash it all in and retire at a Club Med somewhere?"

"You don't sound like a cop."

"I don't think like one, either. They don't pay me enough. Why you think I fell in with Fell? We had a deal 'cause he didn't trust you. You like that little fight we staged out near the piers? Think the two of *you* cooked it up for *my* benefit? Hell, Eddie and I would have been long gone with that container if Sigi hadn't beat us to it."

"You've got no leverage, Squire."

"I've got a truck just outside that'll haul this container into the void. And about two minutes in which to do it, is my guess. You can have Eddie's share and the cops'll have another unsolved murder. So what's the verdict, Paul? If I were you I wouldn't dwell on it."

He dwells on it anyway, for a few seconds at least. Truth be told, he'd rather blow me away than figure it out. And he still hasn't confessed on video, the cagey bastard.

I say, "What was it about Bailey that got to you, anyway? How'd he come to step on your toes?"

I've derailed him for a few seconds more. Behind me I can sense the whir of the video camera.

His voice is vague and flat. "He spotted a weight discrepancy between the manifest out of Hong Kong and the broker filing. Flagged it for inspection and I overrode it."

"And that got him playing detective."

231

He shuts up. What he's said will have to do. Which scarcely matters because DeMarco has made up his mind to kill me. Shoot first, plan later, not like his image at all. Jack Webb would have kept his head.

I'm not thinking any of this clearly. I'm tensing in preparation for diving out of his line of fire, assuming such a thing is possible six feet from the barrel of a .41 Magnum while in handcuffs, which I seriously doubt. But DeMarco isn't paying attention to me anymore. His eyes are trained on the red pinprick of light in the far dark corner of the warehouse. His mouth opens wide.

"Son of a *bitch*!" he says.

I do the dive, but DeMarco's focused on the video camera and doesn't react. I scamper backward on the dirty floor while he goes toward the red light. Shit, I think, can't let him get his hands on that tape. I stagger to my feet and let fly with a running tackle which sends us both plowing into a stack of cartons crammed with bootleg CDs. One of the cartons knocks over the camera, which hits the cement floor with a sickening crack. Another catches DeMarco square on the back of the neck and he makes like Raggedy Andy on the cold hard floor.

I hold my breath, hear nothing. DeMarco isn't moving. The smashed camera lies in one direction, his limp body in the other. I scoot over to him, pivot around on my butt, and start feeling in his jacket for the keys.

They're in the other pocket, the one he's lying on. I plant my hands and vault clumsily over the body. DeMarco groans. I grab his jacket with both hands and heave him onto his back. His eyelids are fluttering and he's beginning to move. His gun isn't in sight.

I hear keys rattling but can't find the right angle. DeMarco makes it harder by trying to turn over. I yank him back, shove a hand into his pocket and grab the keys. A whole lot of keys.

Keys of all shapes and sizes. More than a dozen of them. Five keys, six keys . . . nothing seems to fit. Minutes going by. The next one's a funny shape, like it might fit handcuffs, but I can't find the keyhole. Now DeMarco is sitting up. His eyes go clear. He gets up and slugs me in the stomach. I fall backward on top of my bad arm. Things are getting fuzzy. I'm scratching the hell out of the handcuffs, trying to find the keyhole. DeMarco comes for me again as the key slips in, and turns, and one of the cuffs pops open.

With my arms free I break for the camera. DeMarco grabs my ankle and I go sprawling to within inches of the tripod. I lunge for it as he yanks me off the floor by my collar. I swing wildly with the arm that's still cuffed. The loose ring strikes him in the eye and he screams as I scoop the videotape off the floor. Must have broken free when the camera went flying.

DeMarco loses extra seconds looking for Eddie's gun. Then he remembers the .357 in his jacket. He doesn't give a shit anymore which weapon he uses. By the time he has it out, I'm halfway to the door. He fires and the wall bursts into splinters inches from my head. Then I'm outside, blinded by sunlight, DeMarco on my heels.

I tear off down the street. Jerry's truck is just around the bend. Any second I expect to feel a high-caliber bullet slam into my spine. DeMarco's closing the distance.

I make the turn of the L with a three-length lead. I widen it momentarily by toppling a pair of garbage cans. Time enough to reach Jerry's truck. I yank at the door. It's stuck. I scramble headfirst through the broken window as DeMarco starts peeling off rounds from the .357. They slam into the truck like bazooka shells. I hurl myself across the seat, thrust open the far door and tumble out the other side at precisely the moment that DeMarco's last bullet hits the fuel tank and sends Jerry's truck up in a deafening ball of flame and glass and warped steel.

Thirty-four

■■
■■

IT'S MAGNIFICENT, THIS FIREBALL reaching higher than the
rooftops on either side of the little cul-de-sac. It bursts like
a soap bubble and suddenly it's a hundred little patches of
black smoke and guttering flame. Right away people come
running from all directions, you know the kind, they pop
out of nowhere whenever anything happens. Some plainclothes federal agents pull up, I can tell by the car and the
cut of their suits. Jerry's truck is a smoldering wreck.
DeMarco has disappeared.

My face is hot and my skin's scorched but I'm numb all
over. Eddie's handcuffs dangle from one wrist. In my other
hand is the videotape.

One of the feds spots me and tells his partner to call an
ambulance. He tries to take the tape away but I won't let
him have it. I tell him it's for Detective Lutz, who's with
Homicide. I tell him about the container full of heroin,
which is up for grabs as far as I'm concerned.

The feds turn out to be Eddie's backup, summoned by cell
phone. They had gone to the wrong address.

* * *

Detective Bernard Lutz of Homicide is a tall, distinguished-looking black man with flecks of gray in his hair, a well-groomed mustache and a tiny scar above his left eye. He has on a light gray suit with pale white pinstripes and natural shoulders. His partner is a younger man with freckles and a thatch of red hair. His suit is brown and silky with a fashionably baggy drape. These cops know how to dress.

My own attire consists of a thin white hospital gown with a diagonal pattern of baby blue fleurs-de-lis. My arms are wrapped to the elbows, one's in a cast, and there are Ace bandages around my ribs and left ankle. My face is coated with something greasy and smelly. Plus my eyebrows are missing. Only the arm is broken.

Lutz says, "That's when Fell tried to kill you?"

"No, it was DeMarco tried to kill me. Fell only tried to beat the shit out of me. So far as I can see, Eddie was clean. A little overzealous maybe, but clean."

Customs Inspector Paul E. DeMarco was picked up half an hour after the explosion, wandering around in a daze down by the piers. Cops have spent the last forty-eight hours sorting it out.

Lutz says, "But it was Fell who arranged for the shipment of heroin."

"Maybe, but it was DeMarco's idea. So what if it's a little dicey on the entrapment issue? Leave it to the lawyers to sort out. Eddie was a pretty good cop."

"I'm glad you said that, Jack. Otherwise I might think he was a cop gone bad. Who'd teamed up with a crooked Customs inspector and a cheap con man and murdered an input clerk to protect a forty-million-dollar shipment of heroin."

"You heard what DeMarco said on the tape. That was his doing completely. Eddie and I didn't know about the murder till afterward. Then we didn't have any proof."

"You said on the tape that Fell was dirty."

235

"I was just blowing smoke in DeMarco's face."

"Maybe you're blowing smoke now."

"No, sir. It's a relief to tell the truth at last."

"Uh-huh."

"And by the way, Ray Bailey, he was clean too. You heard what DeMarco said. Write that down in your notebook. That stuff in the papers about his dealing dope was crap."

"Was it?"

"Yeah. All he ever wanted was to be a cop."

"There's the matter of your girlfriend's picture found in his car."

"Okay, that. Sigi, she's the office manager at Morgenstern's, she sent me out to find this lost container. I ran it down, hauled it away and that put Bailey on my trail. He thought I was in on the dope deal, so he busted me. Then it was like I told you."

"And now that container's at the bottom of the bay."

"Courtesy of DeMarco. See for yourself."

"And the broker, this . . . Ingmar Morgenstern."

"I told you about Ingmar. He helped me and Eddie to set up the whole thing. Couldn't have done it without him."

Lutz flips another page in his notebook. Somebody's watching cartoons on a TV across the hall. "And Mr. Frank Thacker?"

Can't give up Thacker without sacrificing Ingmar. A promise is a promise.

"I couldn't say what he was up to," I say. "Conklin and Appelbaum seemed to think he was some sort of a fence, though I never saw any proof of it. I guess he was using me as a decoy, but for what, I don't know. You pick him up yet?"

Lutz and his partner exchange a look. "Word's out to the Coast Guard," Lutz says.

Subject closed. He looks down at his notes and frowns.

"The way you tell it, the pieces fit together. All except for you, Jack. For the life of me I can't figure out what anybody needed you for."

"Like I said, I was sort of a go-between, at least to begin with. I met Sigi in a bar, we got to talking, she offered me a job at Morgenstern's. I was running documents down to the pier because the computer broke down. That's how I met Eddie Fell. He asked me to set up the paperwork with Ingmar. Also to rent a warehouse in order to nail DeMarco."

"You were in handcuffs. He arrested you."

"All that was for DeMarco's benefit. Only Eddie didn't figure that DeMarco would come through the door shooting."

"So a veteran undercover narcotics agent decides to trust a two-bit scam artist out on parole in a sensitive sting operation. Doesn't make a whole hell of a lot of sense."

"He also asked me to set up the video camera."

"I was going to ask you about the video camera."

"That's so it wouldn't be our word against DeMarco's. So we could get him to confess to the murder on tape, just like he did."

Lutz takes a deep breath and studies his notes. He looks to his partner.

"Anything, Rusty?"

Rusty grins tightly. "Oh, no, Bernie. I'm sure Mr. Squire has told us absolutely everything."

Lutz gives me a hard look. "I'm sure he has. 'Cause if we find out he's lying or left something out, and we always do . . . well, his ass would be in a sling. I'm sure he understands that."

"I understand," I say.

Next day Gina comes to see me at the hospital. I've just finished reading an article in the paper about the Coast

237

Guard finding a sleek racing boat about thirty miles off-shore, with no one aboard.

"Fuck, Jack."

"No thanks, Gina. But you could give me a kiss."

"Are you kidding? You look disgusting." *Click.*

"Hey, put down the camera."

"People always say that at the time. Later on they're glad they've got the pictures. Try to smile, okay?"

"If I'm scarred for life, does that mean I don't have to pose in the nude anymore?"

Gina lowers the camera. Her long black hair shimmers like textured silk, not a strand out of place. "No," she says, "this makes it even better. Now shut up and smile."

"Through the pain," I say, even though the drugs have taken care of that. They're also making me woozy. I've been sleeping a lot.

"You bring the package?" I ask her.

She drops a cardboard box on the bed, an eight-inch cube. I place it on the nightstand beside the flower arrangement from Milo.

"Thanks," I say.

She stands two feet from the bed, holding her camera like a shield. Can't decide which way to go.

She says, "Somebody else to see you," and Putz comes through the door in his St. Michael's uniform.

"Putzboy!"

"Hey, Jack." He tosses me a stack of comic books, flops onto the edge of the bed and starts reading one.

"So what do the cops say?" I ask Gina.

Gina hits the auto rewind on her camera. "According to your lawyer you're off the hook on the murder, obviously, and the dope too, although they seem pretty pissed off about that. They don't believe your story about helping the cops but they can't prove otherwise. No chance you'll get away with flattening a cop's motorcycle, though."

"What about Melanie Robinson?"

"Heavy negotiations going on there. What it looks like is, you make restitution on the bike, you get to stay on parole, you lucky fucker."

"People are so tied to material possessions. Do I get my cab back?"

"Didn't ask," Gina says.

I look at Putz. He seems unusually quiet.

"Hey, Putzman. What's happening?"

He mumbles something.

"Say what?"

"I said I told my dad about taking the tray."

"Shit, what happened?"

He shrugs. "Nothing much." He won't look up from the comic he's pretending to read. "He got the tray back out of hock."

"That's it, huh?"

"Pretty much."

"You want me to sic Milo on him or something?"

He shakes his head.

"So, what, you going to stick it out?"

He shrugs again, turns the page.

I have this sudden flash of being thirteen. It's not a vision exactly, not anything I can get my arms around. It's more like a smell, an atmosphere from a long time ago. Then *poof*, it's gone. Must be the drugs.

I look at Putz, sitting on the edge of the hospital bed, deep in his comic book. Gina's staring at me with her eyebrows raised. I say, "Listen, kid. You need help on anything, anytime, you let me know, okay?"

Another shrug.

"What I'm saying is, if it comes to that, you come to me. You hear what I'm saying, man?"

"Yeah. Sure, Jack."

"I mean it. Like Captain America and Bucky Barnes."

"Okay." Putz turns away, a little embarrassed.

Gina's wearing a strange expression. "Well," she says. "Gotta go."

Putz's face brightens. "Gina and I are having dinner together." His lovestruck puppy act.

"Gina . . ."

"I'm fucking starving," she says. "So long, Jack."

I was about to suggest Chinese takeout in the hospital room.

Gina's almost out the door when she turns and comes back to my bed. She leans over and gives me a long kiss.

"Get well quick, you piece of shit," she says.

Affectionately.

It's 9 P.M. and I'm watching a show about a grizzled old cop and a hotheaded young cop busting up a Colombian drug ring operating out of a thirty-minute lube joint. The music's kicking up and the big shootout is about to begin when Jerry Mack's head appears in the doorway.

"Hey, Jer. Don't be shy, man, come all the way in."

He does it a piece at a time. He's wearing black work pants and a windbreaker over a T-shirt and clutching a baseball cap.

"Jack."

"Sit down, Jer. Have some Jell-O. How 'bout those Marauders?"

He shakes his head, watches TV for a moment.

I say, "Good news about the truck, huh? Lucky you kept up your premiums."

Jerry's old truck is a total loss, but it was insured to the max. That's Jerry for you. Mr. Responsibility.

"Gonna take 'em a couple weeks to replace it," he says.

"Yeah, all that red tape. But you could use the time off. You've been working hard."

"I guess so."

"Melanie off your back?"

"She didn't say nothing. I guess she's still gonna let me move."

"She's not so hard to handle when you know how. Anyway, your truck went down for a good cause. She can't argue with that."

Jerry grunts.

"A goddamn blaze of glory, Jer. You should have been there."

I'm trying to keep it light because I can tell he's still depressed. I'd feel the same way if the Checker blew sky-high, never mind the reason. For a guy like Jerry, that truck was his best friend. Be a while before he warms up to the new one.

I've stalled long enough. This will cheer him up.

I reach for the box at bedside that Gina dropped off.

"Here, Jer. Little present for you."

Jerry turns over the box in his hands.

"Go ahead, open it."

He rips it open, unwraps the tissue paper.

And pulls out a chrome bulldog, a shiny new Mack truck hood ornament.

"A brand new start, Jerry."

Who said Jack Squire doesn't keep his promises?

Right up here okay?

Don't mean to rush but there's another electroplaters' convention in town. Figure I'll drop by for a free lunch and a run around the exhibit hall. Never know what you'll find. Something always comes up.

Hell of a cab, isn't it? Not like one of those plastic go-carts they make today. You feel safe in this one.

That'll be thirty-seven fifty.

Didn't I say it would be on the meter?

Yeah, well, inflation, you know? Books aren't a whole lot cheaper.

Exit curbside, please. I'm not insured.

Lousy tipper.